The sergeant's voice is hoarse and barely audible as he relates his tale. 'Creatures... Kappa... came out of the sea and attacked us. Taken by surprise... Only a few of us got away. Master Giru set up a camp in the old palace ruins... The Kappa patrols are scouring the city...'

With the last of his strength, the dying sergeant pulls you closer. 'They're after the Eye of the Dragon. You have to stop them...'

Gamebooks from Fabled Lands Publishing

by Jamie Thomson and Dave Morris:
Fabled Lands 1: The War-Torn Kingdom
Fabled Lands 2: Cities of Gold and Glory
Fabled Lands 3: Over the Blood-Dark Sea
Fabled Lands 4: The Plains of Howling Darkness
Fabled Lands 5: The Court of Hidden Faces
Fabled Lands 6: Lords of the Rising Sun

by Dave Morris:
Heart of Ice
Down Among the Dead Men
Necklace of Skulls
Once Upon a Time in Arabia
Crypt of the Vampire
The Temple of Flame
The Castle of Lost Souls

by Oliver Johnson:
Curse of the Pharaoh
The Lord of Shadow Keep

by Dave Morris and Oliver Johnson
Blood Sword 1: The Battlepits of Krarth
Blood Sword 2: The Kingdom of Wyrd
Blood Sword 3: The Demon's Claw
Blood Sword 4: Doomwalk

by Jamie Thomson and Mark Smith:
Way of the Tiger 1: Avenger
Way of the Tiger 2: Assassin
Way of the Tiger 3: Usurper
Way of the Tiger 4: Overlord
Way of the Tiger 5: Warbringer
Way of the Tiger 6: Inferno
Falcon 1: The Renegade Lord

In preparation
Blood Sword 5: The Walls of Spyte

The Eye of the Dragon

DAVE MORRIS

First published 1985 by Grafton Books

This edition published 2016 by Fabled Lands Publishing,
an imprint of Fabled Lands LLP

www.sparkfurnace.com

ISBN-13: 978-1-909905-28-3
ISBN-10: 1-909905-28-3

To M. A. R. Barker

CHARACTER SHEET

VIGOUR	Current score:	**ITEMS**
AGILITY	Current score:	Orb of Illumination sword 10 gold pieces hipflask of fresh water
PSI	Current score:	

SPELLS

1 Burning Tiger
2 Befuddle
3 Gust of Wind
4 ESP
5 Mind Shield
6 Mirage
7 The Deadly Swarm
8 Séance
9 Dagger of the Mind
10 Invulnerability
11 Dodge
12 Healing

OPPONENTS

VIGOUR	*VIGOUR*
VIGOUR	*VIGOUR*
VIGOUR	*VIGOUR*

INTRODUCTION

Imagine how it would feel to be Katniss Everdeen, or Jon Snow, or Odysseus. Rather than merely sitting back and watching somebody else's adventures, the thrill and danger would be yours to experience at first hand. Only your own skill and daring, and the decisions you made, would stand between you and a hundred hideous deaths.

In Golden Dragon Gamebooks, *you* are the hero.

You are a noble of the Elder Realm, a legend-shrouded kingdom in which the elite are taught the twin arts of sorcery and swordplay. You are one of the most skilled of all the Warrior Mages, but you found life in the idyllic Elder Realm too unexciting for your tastes, so you have spent the last few years adventuring through other lands. You have fought with giants, dragons, warlocks and other terrifying opponents. With each new victory or daring escapade, your reputation has grown. Now you are widely sought after, showered with offers of gold and gems if only you will undertake one perilous mission or another.

To determine just how good an adventurer you are, you must use the dice:

Roll three dice. Add 20 to this number and enter the total in the VIGOUR box on your Character Sheet. This score represents your strength, fitness and general will to survive. Any wounds you take during your quest are subtracted from your VIGOUR score. If it ever reaches zero you are dead.

Roll one die. Add 3 to the number rolled and enter the total in the PSI box on your Character Sheet. The higher this score, the better you are at resisting spells cast at you and the more sensitive you are to psychic impressions.

Roll one die, add 3 and enter the total in the AGILITY box. This score reflects how nimble you are. You will need a high AGILITY to scale walls, leap across chasms, and so on.

You can keep your scores on this Character Sheet in pencil so that they can be erased for further adventures, or you may prefer to make a new copy each time.

YOUR NAME

It will help to make your adventure that much more exciting if you can really make your adventuring self come alive. Try to think of an heroic name. You are a Warrior Mage of the Elder Realm, so perhaps you could call yourself Ragnor Runesword, or Helgrim the Warlock, or Sir Inconnu, or Morgan le Fay. Or, in fact, whatever name suits the image you have conjured up for yourself.

VIGOUR, AGILITY and PSI

Your VIGOUR will change constantly during the adventure—every time you are wounded, in fact. One of your spells, Healing, will restore some lost VIGOUR points—but it will not increase your VIGOUR above its original value. This is your normal VIGOUR score, and you must keep a careful note of it.

Your AGILITY and PSI are less likely to change, although this is possible. Spraining your ankle, for example, might reduce your AGILITY by 1 point. A magic helmet might increase your PSI (or decrease it, if the helmet were cursed). But, as with VIGOUR, your AGILITY and PSI will never exceed their normal scores unless you are specifically told otherwise.

COMBAT—HOW TO FIGHT THE DENIZENS OF THE RUINED CITY

During the course of your adventure, you will often come across a monster or human enemy whom you must fight. When this happens, you will be presented with an entry something like the following:

The Vampire pulls a gleaming scimitar from his belt and stalks towards you, baring his fangs in an evil smile. There is nowhere to run—you must fight.

VAMPIRE   VIGOUR 15

Roll two dice:

score 2 to 6	You are hit and lose 3 VIGOUR points
score 7 to 12	The Vampire loses 3 VIGOUR points

If you kill him, turn to **169**.

At the start of every combat, you should record your opponent's VIGOUR score in an empty Encounter Box. You then begin the combat by rolling two dice and, as indicated in the entry, taking the appropriate number of points from either your own or your enemy's VIGOUR score. You repeat this procedure for successive Combat Rounds, deducting VIGOUR points each time, until the VIGOUR score of either you or your opponent is reduced to—indicating death.

ESCAPING FROM COMBAT

In some cases you may be engaged in combat and find yourself losing. If given the option, you can *flee* from the combat. Your enemy will, however, attempt to strike a blow at your unguarded back as you turn to run. To represent this, whenever you choose to *flee* you should roll two dice and compare the total to your AGILITY score. If the dice roll exceeds your AGILITY then you have been hit (losing 3 VIGOUR points) as you *flee* but if the roll is less than or equal to your AGILITY then you dodge your opponent's parting blow and escape without further injury.

SPELLS

Your magical training provides you with twelve magic spells that will prove invaluable to you on your quest. In most cases, you may cast a spell only when presented with the option to do so. However, some of the spells (the last four on your list) can be cast whenever you need them.

Each of your spells can be used only *once* during the adventure. When you cast a spell, you must remember to cross if off the list on your Character Sheet so that you do not inadvertently try to use it again.

Your spells are:

1. *Burning Tiger*

Your most powerful combat-oriented spell. This will summon a creature of living flame to do battle for you. It will also perform other services—but these reluctantly, because it prefers to fight. The Burning Tiger will remain in existence for only a short time (long enough to defeat most opponents, however) and will then return to its own world.

2. *Befuddle*

This spell has the effect of confusing a creature—it may wander off, drop an item, forget to fight you, etc. Befuddle must be used wisely, as it only affects creatures which are fairly dim-witted in the first place.

3. *Gust of Wind*

Not the most powerful spell at your disposal, but one which can prove a life-saver if used at the right moment. It creates a momentary and very powerful gale blowing away from you in any direction you wish.

4. *ESP*

This detects the presence of thoughts within a range of about ten metres. It lasts for only a few moments, but this is generally long enough for you to tell whether the thoughts are those of humans, goblins or whatever. Animals do not register on this spell.

5. *Mind Shield*

This spell is used to protect your mind when you are attacked by hypnosis or other kinds of mental assault.

6. *Mirage*

With this spell you can create a single illusion of anything you can visualize, so long as it is no bigger than man-sized. The illusion lasts for about a minute—usually long enough for you to dupe someone, or decoy a foe while you escape.

7. *The Deadly Swarm*

A simple but powerful spell for use in battle. The spell creates a swarm of angry hornets which will attack whoever you command them to. Like the Burning Tiger, these insects remain in the real world for only the half minute or so that the spell lasts.

8. *Séance*

A necromantic spell that is not to be used lightly. It causes the ghost of a dead person to materialize before you and answer your questions before returning to the Afterlife. You may only use this spell to summon the ghost of someone known to you, or whose dead body you have come across during your mission. Be warned: use of this spell may prove harrowing or even dangerous if you raise a hostile ghost.

9. *Dagger of the Mind*

When you cast this spell, a glowing dagger appears in the air nearby and shoots unerringly to strike the target you choose. You can use it at the start of any combat to inflict the automatic loss of 3 VIGOUR points on your enemy. Certain non-combat uses of the spell will occasionally be given as options during the adventure.

10. *Invulnerability*

Unfortunately, the type of invulnerability conferred by this spell lasts for only a few seconds. You can use it during any combat to prevent yourself from taking a wound indicated by a Combat Roll—that is, to negate the loss of VIGOUR points in one Combat Round only.

It will not protect you for the whole of the battle. You can also cast it when you choose to *flee*, or whenever it is presented as an option during the adventure.

11. *Dodge*

You can use this spell at any time when you are called upon to make an AGILITY roll—that is, to roll two dice and compare the total to your AGILITY. By casting the spell, you eliminate the need to roll the dice and automatically proceed as if you had rolled less than your AGILITY. You can use this spell to avoid an enemy's parting blow when you *flee* from combat.

12. *Healing*

You can cast this spell at any time except when you are in combat. It will restore your VIGOUR score by 15 points—but remember that your VIGOUR can never exceed its normal score, so it is wasteful to use your Healing spell before you have lost at least 15 VIGOUR points.

These, then, are your spells. Bear in mind that you can cast each of them only once during the adventure— knowing the right time to use a particular spell is what distinguishes a master magician from a bumbling apprentice.

ITEMS

While exploring the ruins of Thalios you will doubtless collect a number of items. Some of these may turn out to be useless—even harmful—but sometimes even the most unimportant-looking acquisition may prove vital to your quest. You should fill in items on your Character Sheet as you acquire them and cross them off as they are discarded or used up.

Leaving aside such obvious possessions as your clothing, backpack, etc, which need not be listed, you begin with the following important items which are already listed on your Character Sheet:

your sword
10 gold pieces
the Orb of Illumination
a hipflask containing fresh water

The Orb of Illumination is a magical talisman, hung around your neck, which will produce light whenever you need it. This is clearly a very important item, since most of your adventure will take place within the darkened buildings of Thalios.

THE ADVENTURE

You are now almost ready to begin. You should start by reading the BACKGROUND, then proceed to **1** and to further entries according to the decisions you make.

Be warned: this adventure is difficult, even by the challenging standards set by earlier Golden Dragon Gamebooks. You are highly unlikely to succeed on your first attempt. You have a sketch map of the ruins—use this. Chart out the route you take, map out the interior of any buildings you explore. Note down where you found each item and where you used each spell (and was it the right spell?). If you get killed, fill in a new Character Sheet and try again, using your earlier maps and notes to guide you.

It may take several attempts, but eventually you will win through and rescue the fabulous Eye of the Dragon from the clutches of the inhuman Kappa. And now—your adventure begins.

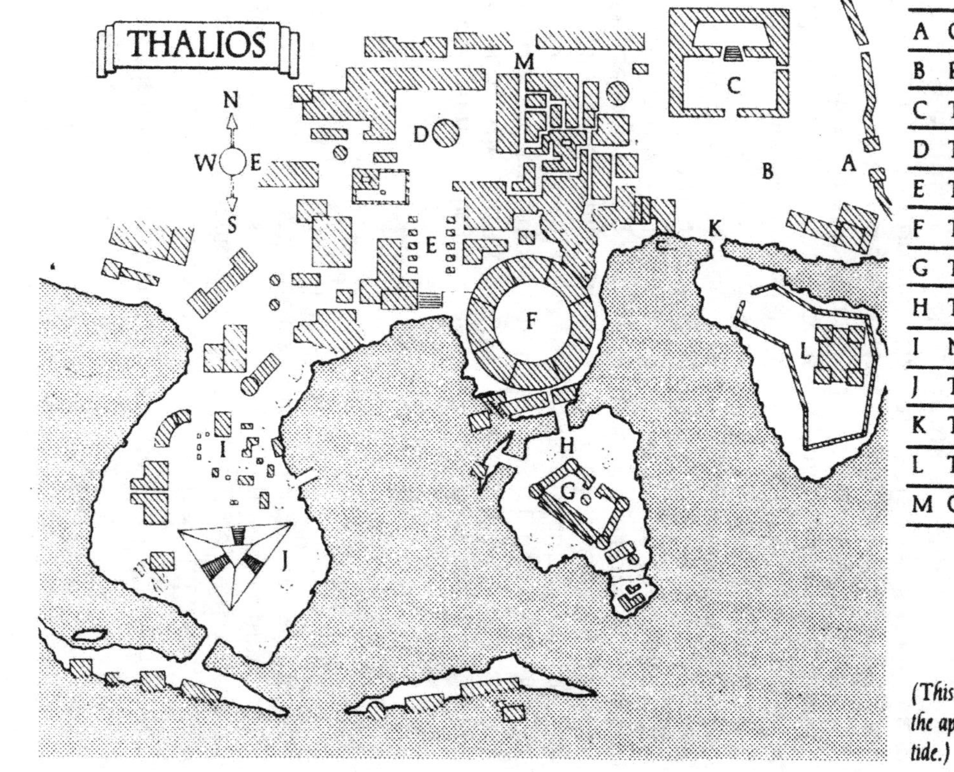

A   City gates
B   Plaza
C   The Temple of Swords
D   The Amber Pantechnicon
E   The Avenue of Sphinxes
F   The Arena
G   The Consul's Palace
H   The Palatine Bridge
I   Necropolis
J   The Vault of Heroes
K   The Bridge of Blue Skulls
L   The Citadel of Conundrums
M   Carfax

(This map shows part of the ruins and the approximate extent of the sea at high tide.)

BACKGROUND

You are seated at one end of a long oak table in the Academy of the Light of Truth, a renowned college in the city of Achtan. Around you sit the High Council of the Academy. In the sallow candlelight, their sombre robes make a striking contrast to the rich azure and gold of your own wizardry regalia. You had intended only to spend a few quiet days in Achtan, but the messenger who brought the High Council's invitation to you at your inn hinted that they might have an interesting mission to offer you. You arrived here a few hours ago to find yourself guest of honour at a superb dinner. Conversation throughout the meal has been urbane and witty, but it has not escaped your notice that they have been subtly quizzing you on your magical abilities. Now that the table has been cleared, you sit back with a goblet of wine in your hand and look around at the wise old faces.

'Rest assured, gentlemen,' you say to them, 'I am indeed, as you have heard, an accomplished Warrior Mage of the Elder Realm.'

They glance at one another and Master Cotullio, a thin man with piercing eyes, leans forward to speak for all of them.

'As you have perceived, our reason for inviting you here was not solely for the sake of your company. Allow me to say that we are indeed honoured to have you as our guest, but I must disclose that we originally acted from an ulterior, though wholly honest, motive. We would like you to undertake a mission for us.'

You savour the wine for a moment. 'You have shown me such hospitality,' you answer suavely, 'that I feel almost obliged to accept. What are the details?'

'Perhaps you know of Thalios,' continues Cotullio. 'A thousand years ago it was a mighty city. The wealth and happiness of its inhabitants made them the envy of the civilized world. Then—disaster. Legends relate that the people of Thalios angered their wrathful gods, or that demons from the sea worked deviltry against them. Whatever the reason, Thalios was wracked by tidal waves and earthquakes which lasted for days and weeks. Those citizens who were not killed at once gathered their belongings and evacuated the city. They were doomed too. Thalios, and with it the land for many leagues all around, began to sink into the sea. The waters rushed in, sweeping across the flats and engulfing the unfortunate evacuees. Today, Thalios is a haunted ruin on the seaward edge of great tidal flats. At low tide it is surrounded by a desolate windswept wilderness. When the sea comes in, the ruins are completely cut off from the mainland by water. Thalios itself lies on higher ground, but much of the city is nonetheless submerged at high tide. It is not an hospitable place.'

'I should venture to agree with you,' you say. 'Why is it of interest?'

'Recently the Academy sent a small archaeological expedition to the ruins. It consisted of only Master Scholar Giru, his assistant, and a few guards such as we normally employ when exploring remote areas. Yesterday, the assistant returned with astounding news. Master Giru has unearthed the Eye of the Dragon.'

You almost let go of your goblet. The Eye of the Dragon is a magical artifact of overwhelming power, mentioned in several ancient texts. You had believed it to be only a fable.

'Master Giru has examined the artifact *in situ*,' Cotullio goes on. 'He reports that there are a host of magical traps and wards protecting the casket which contains it. His opinion is that, if the Eye is to be brought back here, we must engage the services of an experienced sorcerer. Yourself.'

Master Cotullio talks on, explaining that a ship will take you the few days' journey along the coast to the tidal flats, that Giru will meet you at the ruins and take you to the Eye. He hands you a sketch map of the ruins. You take it, only half listening. Your thoughts are ablaze with excitement. You will be the first mortal in ten centuries to gaze upon the legendary Eye of the Dragon!

You accept at once. 'In fact,' you tell the High Council, 'it'll be a pleasant change to take on a mission that doesn't involve even a hint of danger.'

NOW TURN TO 1

1

A ship is chartered to take you some distance along the coast on the first leg of your journey. Your adventure thus begins pleasantly enough—you have nothing to do but bask in the midday sun out on the quarterdeck and watch the crew scurrying about as their gruff captain shouts his orders. The great sail strains in the wind, a block of white against a cloudless sky. Eventually, however, the ship can take you no further. The captain tells you that he is already in dangerously shallow waters, and he is obliged to put you ashore on the tidal flats so that you can walk the rest of the way to Thalios.

Your charts show that you are still some eight miles from the ruins, but it is an easy trek over a seemingly unending expanse of flat wet sands. It is uncanny to imagine how, at high tide in a few hours, the sea will roll in to cover much of the land you are traversing. You begin to glance nervously at the sun as it dips in the sky. If your charts are in error and you cannot find the higher ground where the ruins of Thalios lie...

But no, you see a jagged line of black on the horizon and as you approach the shapes of broken buildings begin to resolve themselves. By the time you reach the city gates, it is almost sunset. The sun shimmers like a ball of fire on the rim of the world. Its light spreads traces of red gold across the embossed armour of four figures who come to greet you as you enter the city. They wear the livery of the Academy, and are presumably an honour guard sent by Master Giru. Nonetheless, you are surprised to see that they have their swords drawn. The sergeant offers no explanation for this, but steps straight up to you saying, 'Come with us. We will take you to Giru.'

Something in their manner makes you suspicious. Will you go with them (turn to **31**), decline, saying you will find Master Giru yourself (turn to **227**), or draw your sword and attack them (turn to **53**)?

2

Do you have a small ivory Arena ticket? If so, turn to **178**. If you are not a ticket holder, turn to **203**.

3

You feint and quickly dodge back away from the sluggish bulk of the Kraken. Before it can lash out, you have plunged under the icy water and are groping your way along the submerged tunnel as quickly as you can go. You had no time to take a deep breath, and your lungs are soon bursting. At last you reach the end of the tunnel. When your head breaks the surface and you gasp in fresh air, you give a silent prayer of thanks. Taking stock of your new surroundings, you see that you are in some sort of enclosed courtyard in the middle of the mansion. The open night sky is above you. It will take you some time to scale the sheer walls surrounding the courtyard, but—

These thoughts are cut short as a pulpy grip closes around your ankle. You shudder with fear. You did not imagine for one moment that the dread Kraken would be able to follow you along the narrow tunnel. Somehow it has done just that, and is squeezing its bloated body out into the half-submerged courtyard. You must fight it; there is now nowhere to run.

Roll two dice:

score 2 to 3	Turn to **125**
score 4 to 6	You are hit several times; roll two dice and deduct that many VIGOUR points
score 7 to 12	The Kraken loses 3 VIGOUR

If you kill it, you return along the tunnel to the cellar: turn to **271**.

4

You rush through the gaping entrance and across the shadowy hall to the double doors. As you fumble with these, you glance back to see the shambling statue looming in dim silhouette on the moonlit porch. The doors come open and you dash through. The ringing metallic footfalls are close behind, and you have to quell your racing heart long enough to walk slowly across the creaking plank.

If your current AGILITY is less than 4, turn to **143**. If your current AGILITY is 4 or greater, turn to **52**.

5

Given no other choice, you rush at the two Kappa with your sword raised high to strike. Their baroque coral faces show no expression, but in their stance you read alarm and perhaps fear.

FIRST KAPPA   VIGOUR 9
SECOND KAPPA   VIGOUR 12

Roll two dice:
score 2 to 4   You are hit twice; lose 6 VIGOUR
score 5 to 7   You are hit once; lose 3 VIGOUR
score 8 to 12   One of the Kappa (you decide which) loses 3 VIGOUR

If you slay one of them, turn to **239**.

6

Chu switches the inverted shells around with blurring speed, but you are fairly sure that you know which one the pearl is under. He looks up at you smugly. If you point to the shell you have your eye on, turn to **286**. If you cheat with a Mirage spell (assuming you have not already cast it earlier in the adventure), turn to **261**.

7

What item will you use:

A flask of fresh water?   Turn to **22**
A Wristband of Fire?   Turn to **9**
A set of black leather reins?   Turn to **70**

If you do not have any of these, you must draw your sword and fight: turn to **50**.

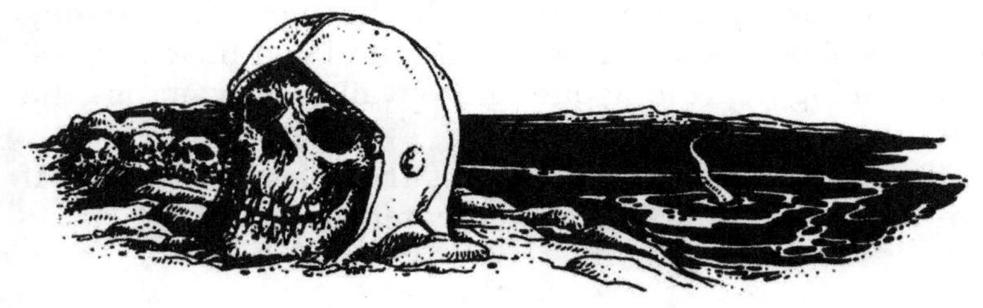

8

The other Kappa screams as it presses the attack. It is an unearthly and desolate sound.

Roll two dice:
score 2 to 5   You are hit; lose 3 VIGOUR
score 6 to 12   The Kappa loses 3 VIGOUR

If you win, turn to **44**.

9

The wristband hurls a globe of snarling flame towards the monstrous demon. He rears up and shouts into the wind. Immediately a high wave crashes on to the beach, dousing the fire you have created. Nuckelavee's laughter is a foul jeering cacophony.

You cannot use the wristband again—all its power is now expended. As Nuckelavee gallops out of the water to attack, you barely have time to draw your sword.

Turn to **50**.

10

Streaks of flame appear in the air and coalesce to form a tiger of living fire. It roars like a furnace and leaps to intercept the Kappa before they can reach you. Their unearthly cries pierce the night as the tiger cuts sizzling globules of molten coral from their bodies with each swipe of its claws. Soon the tiger fades away, leaving the bridge strewn with the horribly dismembered remains of two coral corpses.

Turn to **44**.

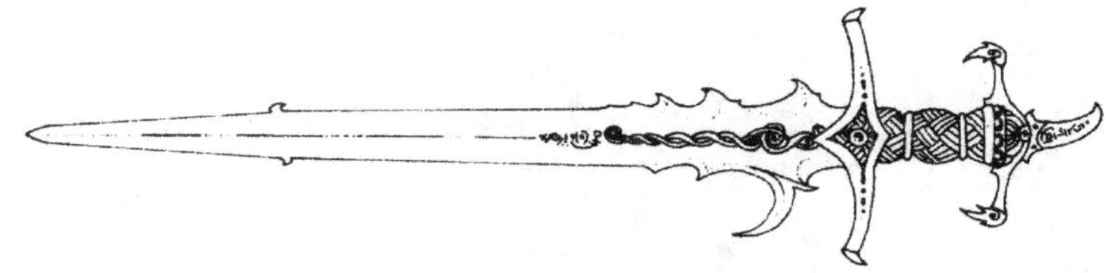

11

The other lich knight gives vent to a horrible scream as its comrade topples off the bank into the water. You seem to sense Death at your shoulder, to hear his soft sere chuckle in your ear. You somehow find the strength to battle on.

Roll two dice:
score 2 to 6   You are wounded; lose 3 VIGOUR
score 7 to 12   The lich knight loses 3 VIGOUR

If you win, turn to **142**.

12

The entrance to the Arena is a massive arched tunnel. It is said that competitors in the chariot races could ride in three abreast, and looking at the size of the tunnel you find this easy to believe. You head along it, feeling sheltered by the darkness. Doors on either side lead up to the stands, but you carry straight on to the end and emerge into the Arena. On the far side—almost a hundred metres from where you are standing—is another, identical tunnel. Your map suggests you have found an ideal short cut to the Palatine Bridge.

You glance around at the monumental sweeping tiers of marble seats, imagining the cheering crowds that once pressed into them. You can almost hear the echo of their surging roar as they thrilled to the Arena's spectacular displays. Could anything in those far-off days compare to the adventure in which you are now embroiled? You shrug. They are all dust on the wind

now, those teeming multitudes of ancient Thalios. Not even their ghosts remain. The only symbol of that lost glory is a giant winged statue on a soaring pedestal above the Judicial Box.

No Kappa are in sight. You slip from the shadows and dash across the floor of the Arena. Turn to **2**.

13

There is a moment of darkness and disorientation. It passes, and you find yourself standing before a gimlet-eyed sorcerer clad in linen and gilded finery. His face is pale, and you think you see him tremble as he looks upon you.

'Who are you?' you demand of him. 'How do you come to be here?' Your voice seems chill and unemotional. Something is wrong, but you cannot quite tell what.

The sorcerer supplies the answer. 'It is I who ask the questions,' he says, visibly unnerved. 'You are here only by the power of my Séance spell. You died centuries ago, from eating poisoned fruit...'

Your adventure is over.

14

This is no time for subtlety. You must attack the monster with one of your most powerful enchantments—either Burning Tiger (turn to **191**), the Deadly Swarm (turn to **98**) or Befuddle (turn to **174**). If you have already cast all of these, turn to **92**.

15

They chortle eerily and produce a hexagonal board inscribed with six symbols—a wand, an hourglass, a dagger, a broken alembic, a hooked staff and a knapsack. One of the gloomviles takes a severed finger from a box and drops it in the middle of the board. He explains that to play the game you must prod this finger, which will then writhe around in a circle until it comes to rest pointing at one of the symbols. An appropriate effect will then result, depending on the symbol indicated.

To play the game you must have at least one spell left, and at least one item in your possession apart from your sword and the Orb of Illumination. If you do not meet these requirements, return to **42** and choose another game. If you are able to play Finger of Fate, you reach out and touch the severed finger. It immediately begins to turn and flop about obscenely. 'The moving finger writhes,' titters a gloomvile.

Where does it come to rest? Roll one die:

1	The Wand	Regain one of the spells you have used. You chose which one. (If you have not yet used any spells, nothing happens).
2	The Hourglass	Turn to **226**
3	The Dagger	Lose 3 VIGOUR points
4	The Alembic	Lose one of your spells (you can choose which).
5	The Staff	Gain 3 VIGOUR points.
6	The Knapsack	One of your items vanishes. You decide which, though it must not be your sword or the Orb.

If you are still alive after one game, and still eligible to play, you may have another go. Once you have had enough of Finger of Fate, you can return to **42** and choose a different game or else continue on your way by turning to **208**.

16

You tinker with the strings of the harp, but you cannot seem to produce quite the note you want.

If you have them, you can now try a silver figurine (turn to **246**), a tuning fork (turn to **81**) or an unidentified potion (turn to **65**). Otherwise, you can continue on your way (turn to **288**).

17

The plank creaks alarmingly as you cross, but manages to bear your weight. There is a trickle of cold sweat on your brow by the time you reach the other side of the pit.

Your magical illumination pushes back the shadows. A large white mask hangs ahead of you at the end of a gallery of polished blue-black stone. It wears a tragic expression. However, as you move along the gallery towards it, the blindly staring eyes of the mask suddenly glow and the expression changes from tragedy to hellish glee. Its chilling battle-shriek roots you to the spot, and in that moment you know it for what it is. You are under attack from a prosopteryx—not a mask at all, but a huge flying parody of a human head. It comes rushing through the air towards you, rapidly extending the mane of sharp corundum spines with which it intends to slash you to ribbons.

Will you meet it with drawn sword (turn to **43**), or will you cast a spell (turn to **26**)?

18

You pass through the gateway in the high wall into a courtyard. Bamboo grows thickly here above the level of your head, and you easily conceal yourself until the solitary Kappa has gone by.

If you struggle through the overgrown courtyard towards the main building, turn to **36**. If you go back out on to the deserted plaza, turn to **274**.

19

The spell does not stop the shrieks and wails that fill your ears, but at least the feeling of clammy terror departs. Enclosed by your tiny circle of light, you walk slowly along the benighted hall.

Suddenly a hideous scream erupts from right beside you. Lank, ragged arms reach into the light and try to grasp you with claw-like hands. You catch a glimpse of leering deaths-head faces on the edge of darkness.

Stifling a cry, you blunder on and discover you have reached the far end of the hall. It seems to have taken you an eternity. You climb the steps out of the horrible darkness, certain that if not for your Mind Shield you would now be a quivering lunatic.

Turn to **259**.

20

You find a point where the high wall around the Citadel has fallen in. Clambering over this, you discover the sea lapping in along the pebble beach with a calming sigh. But as you look at the breaking waves, you find yourself imagining legions of Kappa troops waiting to emerge from the fastnesses of their oceanic realm, to rise out of the water and spread bloodshed and terror.

You glance up at the moon, now a watery pearl behind a fine pall of drizzle. Gargantuan clouds slide imperceptibly across the sky. Somewhere in the ruined city, is Master Giru watching the same moon, waiting to guide you to the Eye of the Dragon? Or have the Kappa already found him and dragged him with them beneath the waves? You must pray for the former, and try to locate him with all speed.

Across a hundred metre stretch of water you can see the Consul's Palace. If you wish to cross over to it then a boat would be useful—but there is none in sight. Will you walk south along the shore in search of one (turn to **72**), or will you stay here and try to think of another way to get across the bay (turn to **179**)?

21

You can cast either an ESP spell (turn to **200**) or a Gust of Wind spell (turn to **112**).

22

You hurriedly unstopper the flask and shower Nuckelavee's skinless body with the contents. You see his grotesque flank pucker and shrivel as the water burns him like acid. His bellow of agonized rage strikes terror into your quaking heart. He plunges back into the safety of the cool sea water and, maddened by pain, begins to thrash about in an effort to wash off the searing unsalted water.

You are ready with your sword, but Nuckelavee has lost his taste for battle. He glares redly at you, screams an ugly curse, and sinks beneath the black waves.

Turn to **183**.

23

'Pizh and tozh!' exclaims Lord Mantiss as you hold up the item you have chosen. 'That iz a cherizhed heirloom. Anything elze, you could have taken with my blezzingz— but now, I regret to zay, you have offended me.'

Bowed down by what seems to be genuine sorrow, he effortlessly slides the stone block back into place across the doorway. You curse and yell at the mad insect-man at the top of your lungs, but there is no reply. You soon realize you will never shift the massive block. For an imagined slight, your deranged captor has condemned you to a slow and lingering death by starvation. You have failed in your quest.

24

You are startled by a movement at the far end of the cellar. A bulky mottled form is rearing up out of the deeper water there. Like an octopus, its arms sway up to cast a net of shadows on the ceiling. But it is not an octopus that surges forth into the gleam of your Orb of

Illumination. On each of its tentacles is a clutching hand. Its body is like a deformed skull with rolling yellow eyes. It is the Kraken, a supernatural horror which lurked in the catacombs of Thalios even in ancient times. You have invaded its millennial slumber, and it intends to rend you limb from limb.

If you cast a spell, turn to **129**. Otherwise turn to **110**.

25

You lift the wooden flask to your lips and drink. Almost at once, all sensation of weight leaves you as the magical potion annuls the force of gravity upon your body. You start to walk west across the stretch of water separating you from the Consul's Palace. Your feet tread softly on air, a couple of inches above the swelling waves. Abruptly you realize that your weight is returning—the potion's effects are wearing off, and you are not much more than halfway across the bay. Seeing the shadowy bulk of a sandbank which juts out from the far shore, you hurry towards it. You breathe a sigh of relief as you reach it just in time.

Turn to **156**.

26

Which spell will you try:

Gust of Wind?	Turn to **292**
The Deadly Swarm?	Turn to **245**

If you have already cast both of these, turn to **43**.

27

As you walk down the steps it is like entering an icy pool. You shiver from the coldness and from a sensation of imminent malevolence. The light of your magical Orb of Illumination penetrates no more than a few metres into the darkness, which does not seem to be a mist but rather a zone of zero light. There is a tight knot of panic in the pit of your stomach as you begin to edge along the hall. A low moaning drifts out of the blackness all around you. It seems to come from very far away. Mad cackling cries approach and recede, circle about you. You advance blindly. Onto the wall of darkness beyond the Orb's meagre light, your mind projects all manner of imagined terrors. Your flesh crawls with a feeling of dread. The terrible fear builds to screaming pitch, and you realize that unless you use your Mind Shield spell you may go mad.

If you cast the spell, turn to **19**. If not, will you turn back and try to find the way out (turn to **47**) or will you press on regardless (turn to **287**)?

28

You push your way south against a gale that throws sharp needles of icy rain into your face. To either side, a line of carven sphinxes face one another across the avenue. Their marble bodies are palely luminous in the watery moonlight; their chiselled faces seem grim and brooding. The raindrops could almost be tears on those stone cheeks. You begin to imagine what they must have stared down on through the ages—what secrets would pass their lips if they could talk. But you have no time for such idle fancies now. You hurry on without stopping.

Turn to **210**.

29

The sergeant's fingers close spasmodically on the collar of your robe. His voice is hoarse and barely audible as he relates his tale. 'Evil creatures—Kappa—came out of the sea and attacked us... Many slain... Master Giru set up a camp in the old Consul's Palace, south-west of here... The Kappa patrols are scouring the city... We were sent to escort you to Master Giru, but the Kappa spotted us and one of them used hypnosis...' With the last of his strength, the sergeant pulls you closer. 'Don't let them get the Eye!' he gasps, and then the life goes from him and he falls back.

You cover his body with his cloak as you ponder his last words. You have heard of the Kappa—a heartless eerie race who dwell in undersea fortresses. They hate all other life-forms, and only the opportunity for plunder and killing would bring them on to land. Some high-ranking Kappa can control men's minds with a hypnotic sorcery, which explains why the unfortunate warriors attacked you. You stand and look out across the city. You will make the Kappa pay for what they have done—but first you must find Master Giru.

Turn to **48**.

30

The tiger appears and licks the metal plate with its fiery tongue. As the plate begins to glow a dull red, your sword drops with a clang to the tunnel floor. You wait for it to cool, by which time the tiger has faded away, then resheathe it and continue on your way.

Turn to **308**.

31

You step warily past the grim-faced sergeant. A moment later you discover your suspicions were justified. His razor-sharp sword bites deep into your shoulder, and you must subtract 3 points from your VIGOUR score. For a moment you watch in disbelief as your blood spurts out on to the wet stones, then you painfully pull your sword from its scabbard.

Turn to **53**.

32

You cast the spell, and slowly a translucent form arises from the pile of bones. You feel the hairs on the nape of your neck bristle; you have never quite got used to this spell. The ghost hangs in the air like a guttering candle-flame, the image of an old wizard in a long gown. 'Let us depart,' it implores in a voice that makes your blood run cold. 'I sense great danger here.'

'You are dead,' you tell the ghost. 'You died many years ago. I have summoned you to give me information.'

'Ah,' sighs the ghost, 'you must go back. Leave this dire place. Here you will find only the remains of brave men, slain by the very essence of nethermost darkness.'

Your glance goes to the mouldering skeleton on the floor. When you look back, the ghost has disappeared. Will you heed its advice and go back downstairs (turn to **88**)? If not, you can open the door (turn to **132**) or continue along the passage (turn to **171**)

33

You can cast either Burning Tiger (turn to **10**) or The Deadly Swarm (turn to **64**), if you have them. If you have already used both these spells, turn to **309** and fight for your life.

34

As you approach the Kappa leader, the force field finally collapses under his magical onslaught. It fades to reveal a small casket on a carved ivory pedestal. The effort of banishing Giru's force field has visibly weakened the Kappa leader. As he sways unsteadily, you leap forward and shoulder him aside. He falls, but as you reach for the casket he catches hold of your robe and pulls you back towards him. His huge pearl eyes seem to glow for an instant, and then a terrible pain stabs through your head. You cover your ears, but you cannot block out the agonizing psionic attack. In a matter of moments he will have enslaved you with his hypnosis.

If you have a bottle of vinegar, turn to **289**. If you would rather rely on your Mind Shield spell, turn to **78**. If you have neither of these, turn to **263**.

35

Do you, in that case, have a golden apple? If so, turn to **68**. If not, turn to **55**.

36

[Illustration on next page]

Your sword quickly cuts a path through the swaying bamboo and you climb the steps of a monolithic grey building that may indeed once have been a temple. You cross the pillared threshold and find yourself in a vast gloomy hall. You call on the magical Orb of Illumination around your neck to give you light to see by. The scene that greets your eyes is one of long neglect. The iron braziers where the eternal flame burned are now cold, and the silver plate armour in which the warrior-god's idol is clad shows a black tarnish. Moonlight slants in through the open colonnade.

If you leave this place and return to the plaza, turn to **274**. If you decide to linger here a while longer, will you place an offering before the idol (turn to **295**), or will you light the braziers (turn to **106**)?

37

Long centuries have passed since Thalios fell to ruin. Many of the derelict buildings have become unsafe. As you cross over towards the mysterious crystal, the roof suddenly caves in beneath you.

You must roll equal to or less than your current AGILITY on two dice. If you succeed, turn to **90**. If the dice roll exceeds your AGILITY, turn to **181**.

38

The chamber in which you find yourself is a place of low vaulted ceilings, shrouded with centuries of dust that

now hangs around you like a mist. You estimate that the chute has carried you into a subterranean section of one of the buildings on the north side of the quadrangle.

The Kappa probably assume you have fallen to your doom, since none has risked pursuing you. In the light of the Orb you see a flight of steps leading up. Eager to get away from the choking clouds of dust, you kick your way through piled boxes full of decaying parchments and begin to ascend the steps.

Turn to **103**.

39

The Kappa holding the sceptre backs away as its companion sweeps gracefully forward to intercept you. You are careful to ensure that the first Kappa gets no opportunity for another clear shot.

KAPPA   VIGOUR 12

Roll two dice:
score 2 to 5   You are hit; lose 3 VIGOUR
score 6 to 12   The Kappa loses 3 VIGOUR

If you kill it, turn to **59**.

40

You sit in the tunnel for a minute, getting your breath back and watching your reptilian tormentor circle fretfully. The empty Arena echoes to its furious cries, but—even though the tunnel is wide enough to accommodate its massive wingspan—it seems to realize that pursuing you now would be foolhardy. At last it returns to perch on the high pedestal and slowly folds its wings. You find yourself wondering if the crowds who flocked to the Arena in centuries past ever witnessed anything like it. Remembering the urgency of your quest, you hurry along the tunnel and out into the street.

Turn to **240**.

41

You reach the weed-choked forecourt of the Citadel. Its heavy bronze doors stand open, enticing you to enter and uncover whatever secrets and treasures lie within. But as you draw closer and gaze into the moonlight shadow beyond the doors, you cannot escape a feeling of dread.

Will you brave the dangers of the Citadel (turn to **102**), or will you take the path down to the western shore of the island (turn to **20**)?

42

Your decision seems to provoke a certain sad joy in the horrible trio. They eagerly bring out dice and tattered rulebooks as you crouch outside the chalked lines of the pentacle. They offer a choice of three games. Which will you play:

Mix-Up?	Turn to **235**
Finger of Fate?	Turn to **15**
Jacks?	Turn to **77**

43

The prosopteryx, its face contorted by a soundless cackle, soars to attack you. You hold your sword ready and concentrate on its darting movements.

PROSOPTERYX   VIGOUR 9

Roll two dice:
score 2 to 6   You are hit; lose 3 VIGOUR
score 7 to 12   The prosopteryx loses 3 VIGOUR

If you *flee* back the way you came, turn to **153**. If you kill it, turn to **119**.

44

You have dealt with their sadistic masters, but you still have the sentinel crabs to contend with. Their eyes wave eerily on stalks as they watch you, clacking their giant pincers together impatiently. As they cluster in towards you, you step back and then suddenly run towards them, leaping so that you land on the back of the nearest one. The other two sweep their claws at your ankles—but the crab on which you are standing, already confused by the weight on its back, assumes they are attacking it. Enraged, it turns on the other two. You make an easy escape, chuckling to yourself at the thought of how simple it was to confound the stupid creatures once their Kappa handlers were out of the way.

You reach the end of the bridge. Turn to **128**.

45

Which will you cast:

Your Burning Tiger spell?	Turn to **157**
Your Deadly Swarm spell?	Turn to **139**

46

The translucent figure of a hard-faced pirate takes shape above the waves in front of you. His velvet coat hangs dankly about him like a grave-sheet. His beard is tangled and matted; it looks like drying seaweed. 'Who is it?' he says in a cold and distant voice. 'Who calls me back to this world when I was being made so comfortable in the next?' He utters a bleak, mirthless laugh.

'I have summoned you,' you call out, keeping your voice loud to mask a slight tremor of unease, 'and I command you. I desire to cross this bay to reach the ancient palace yonder. If you know of a means by which I can do this, I now require you to speak.'

'Command me?' snarls the ghost. 'No man commanded Black Jack Tar when he lived, damn your eyes. Go for my boat, moored to the jetty just south of here. The oars are hidden under a thicket nearby.' He begins to shiver and fade. 'I'll see you soon enough in hell, you lily-livered landlubber…'

The voice trails off and is lost on the sea breeze. Turn to **220**.

47

Somehow you find your way back to the steps and escape from the stygian darkness. Your harrowing experience has left you weak and trembling—lose 1 VIGOUR point. You stare across the impenetrable blackness to where the bowl lies gleaming in the dull red light. Doubtless it holds some tempting treasure, but nothing could induce you to go back into that twittering darkness. After resting for a moment or two to get a grip on yourself, you leave the room and walk along the passage.

Turn to **171**.

48

You move hastily across the plaza. The ancient flagstones are cracked and broken and slimy with algae, and there are numerous shallow pools of water where the ground has subsided. Sunset is no more than a crimson blaze in the western sky. The lengthening shadows are turning to night. Soon the moon will be up—bringing with it, of course, the tides. At high tide many of the streets will lie underwater, making your passage through Thalios much more difficult. You must hope to find Master Giru within a few hours.

You stop and shrink back into the darkness beside a fallen column as you catch sight of a tall figure in the distance. It is very thin, vaguely manlike but with many -jointed limbs which posture jerkily as it moves. In the twilight you can see that its huge eyes are lambent white pearls, and its body is an open latticework of coral. A Kappa!

It is moving straight towards where you are hiding. Will you dodge through the gateway of the building next to you, marked on your map as the Temple of Swords— turn to **18**? Or will you wait for the Kappa to draw level with you and then attack it—turn to **268**?

49

The leathery monster cannot manoeuvre on the ground, but its panic drives it into a frenzied bloodlust and it fights you with all the savagery of a primitive beast at bay.

FLYING REPTILE   VIGOUR 12

Roll two dice:
score 2 to 5   You are wounded and lose 3 VIGOUR
score 6 to 12   The flying reptile loses 3 VIGOUR

If you kill it, you continue across to the opposite side of the Arena. Turn to **240**.

50

Nuckelavee fends your first blow aside with a powerful kick. His hoofs send a shrieking rain of sparks from your sword-blade. For all your skill, you are only a mortal—but Nuckelavee, he is the Demon Lord of the Ocean.

NUCKELAVEE   VIGOUR 21

Roll two dice:
score 2 to 8   You are struck—lose 4 VIGOUR
score 9 to 12   Nuckelavee loses 3 VIGOUR

There is no point in trying to *flee*. Nuckelavee would never permit you to get away now that you have had the temerity to attack him. If you win, turn to **183**.

51

The door opens and you step into a narrow room. The air reeks of brine and the walls sparkle with a mantle of caked salt; it reminds you of hoarfrost. Across the room, beyond a stout iron grating, you see a set of black leather reins hanging from a hook on the wall. You examine the grating. It is firmly secured and the bars are far too strong for you to stand any chance of bending them.

Do you have an unidentified potion in an alabaster jar? If so, turn to **137**. If not, you leave the room and go down the passage opposite: turn to **93**.

52

On the far side of the yawning pit, you turn to await your implacable pursuer. The massive statue stoops to pass through the double doors. Its soulless eyes are fixed upon you and it does not even pause at the pit's edge. The moment that it steps out on to the plank, the rotted wood splinters and gives way under its weight. The statue seems almost to hang suspended for an instant as it slowly topples forward. Without a sound, it drops into the yawning darkness. Glancing off the rusted spikes, it is swallowed up by the oily waters. The broken halves of the plank follow it down and are carried away by the current.

Although you have overcome the bronze statue, you are now confronted with a new problem: how will you get back across the pit? If you have a Potion of Wind Walking, turn to **111**. If not, turn to **134**.

53

There is a strange murderous glint in the eyes of the four men. They are either mad or under magical control.

SERGEANT	VIGOUR 12
FIRST WARRIOR	VIGOUR 9
SECOND WARRIOR	VIGOUR 9
THIRD WARRIOR	VIGOUR 9

Roll two dice:

score 2	You are hit four times—lose 12 VIGOUR
score 3 to 4	You are hit three times—lose 9 VIGOUR
score 5 to 6	You are hit twice—lose 6 VIGOUR
score 7	You are hit once and lose 3 VIGOUR
score 8 to 12	One of them (you choose which) loses 3 VIGOUR

Once you have defeated one, turn to **196**. (Make sure you have recorded the remaining VIGOUR scores of the other three first, however).

54

Alert for other patrols, you creep swiftly across the quadrangle and into the deep shadows beside the Pantechnicon. Valuable artifacts of many kinds were once stored within this colossal building. Some of them may have been magical. You cannot see any sign of such treasures when you peer between the bars of the huge gate—just the inky blackness of the interior. A lone albatross gives a mournful cry as it wheels across the night sky. You hesitate for only a moment before hauling the gate open. The screech of rusty hinges echoes back loudly from the buildings all around the quadrangle. You wince and, hoping that there are no Kappa nearby to have heard the noise, hurry inside.

Turn to **192**.

55

Giru places his hands on the table in a gesture of resignation. 'There is nothing here that we can use to reach the Eye,' he says sadly. 'The Kappa will soon claim it and take it back to their undersea kingdom. We have failed.'

The four of you sit in silence, heads bowed dejectedly. In a few hours the Kappa will have left Thalios and you can return home safely. But that is small compensation for the fact that, despite the many dangers you have faced and overcome, you have not been able to prevent the evil Kappa from getting the Eye of the Dragon. Your mission ends in bitter failure.

56

A few ancient characters are engraved into the face of the plaque. You are not much of a classicist, but you eventually decipher the words Admit One'. Then you remember that the people of Thalios used pieces of ivory as tickets to the Arena.

You slip the ticket into a pocket of your robe and cross over to the door. Turn to **208**.

57

You shrug off the effects of the mysterious spell, but the strain costs you 1 PSI point. You do not wait around to find out what other spells the spider has at its command. You hurl yourself through the doorway and run on along the corridor.

Turn to **288**.

58

Your spell throws the heavy gate of the Pantechnicon shut, hurling the Kappa off-balance into the. hall. You can now either attack them (turn to **39**) or escape (turn to **116**).

59

Throughout your battle, the other Kappa has been standing in the entrance to the Pantechnicon, calling out for reinforcements in the weird ululating wail of this oceanic species. A clamour of answering cries rings out across the empty quadrangle. The Kappa turns, bringing its sceptre round quickly but you are already racing towards the chute in the wall. Hearing the approaching Kappa outside the building, you hurl yourself into the dark opening. Another bolt of crackling energy misses you by inches.

You careen down into darkness, and the piping shouts die away behind you. But relief at your escape quickly changes to alarm. You are on an almost totally frictionless slide, and you are building up considerable momentum. The far end of the chute is rapidly approaching—far too rapidly. Will you brace yourself for the impact (turn to **189**), or attempt to protect yourself with a spell (turn to **214**)?

60

You are being attacked by a sentinel crab. The Kappa train these huge crabs and use them like guard dogs. You draw your sword and fend away the one that has

just wounded you, but even as you do so you see more of the horrible creatures scuttling across the cobblestones towards you. There are too many of them to fight—and rather than waste your spells you decide to run for it. Which way will you go:

South, to the Avenue of Sphinxes?　　Turn to **158**
East, back along the narrow
　alley to the plaza by the Temple
　of Swords ?　　Turn to **85**

61

You have a nagging suspicion in the back of your mind regarding the statue. This is confirmed when a harsh creak breaks the silence and your startled eyes behold the statue slowly coming to life. It clambers ponderously down from its pedestal and trudges heavily towards you. It will be upon you in seconds. Will you fight it (turn to **260**), or turn and run (turn to **223**)?

62

The task of searching for Giru through the labyrinth of halls and corridors within the Palace will not be easy. Like all the nobles of your race, you have a limited sixth sense. This may guide you, but it is neither precise nor reliable. Now is the time to use your Séance spell, if you still have it. Whose ghost will you summon:

One of the warriors who met
　you at the gates of the city?　　Turn to **264**
The man whose mortal remains
　lie at your feet?　　Turn to **89**

If you have already cast the spell, turn to **242**.

63

Are you wearing Mantiss's gauntlet? If so, turn to **121**. If you are not wearing this item, turn to **161**.

<h2 style="text-align:center">64</h2>

You have chosen unwisely. The Kappa's bodies are hard and bony, and they do not even falter as they charge through the cloud of angry hornets conjured up by your spell. Before you can defend yourself, their gleaming scimitars bite into your flesh.

Lose 6 VIGOUR and, if you are still alive, turn to **309**.

<h2 style="text-align:center">65</h2>

You unstopper the jar and drink the mysterious potion. It has a rather syrupy flavour. Within moments you feel your muscles swelling and realize you have just drunk a Potion of Strength. You pound on the door with the might of ten men, but you are unable to force it open. Eventually the magic of the potion wears off—and, with it, your enhanced strength.

If you have a tuning fork, turn to **81**. If not, you decide to continue onwards: turn to **288**.

<h2 style="text-align:center">66</h2>

Despite the pain you do not falter. Ahead looms the tunnel, and safety. You waste no time looking round, but you know that the flying reptile is building altitude for another attack. You hear the slow wing-beats stop as it locks its leathery wings into gliding position and begins its descent. A harsh predatory screech breaks the ominous hush as it plunges down towards you.

Roll three dice, trying to score less than or equal to your current AGILITY. If you succeed, turn to **206**. If you fail, turn to **290**.

67

A spinning orb of yellow-green flame streaks towards you and explodes at your feet. You feel no pain, only a creeping chill through the marrow of your bones. The spider's magic threatens you, and you must use all your psychic strength and training to fight back.

Roll two dice, trying to score less than or equal to your current PSI. If you succeed, turn to **57**. If you fail, turn to **80**.

68

'Why, this is a Proteus fruit!' exclaims Giru. Noticing your blank look, he continues: 'Such fruits transform those who eat them for a short time. I believe the golden variety is exactly what we need.'

You quickly gather up your other items and then the four of you go up to the tower roof. Night is a blue-grey shadow retreating westwards, leaving the eastern sky a pale gold. The tide has gone out from the bay below, leaving a marshy tract of kelp and wet sand. Further west, you can see the promontory where the Vault of Heroes stands. The Vault is a colossal pyramid of ochre stone. Kappa swarm around its base like ants.

Giru hands you the apple and you bite into it. The magic takes effect at once. You begin to shrink. You can feel your bones twisting into new shapes, your muscles shifting under your skin, and feathers sprouting all over your body. There is a look of utter amazement in the faces of the two guards as they watch you change into a proud golden eagle. With a defiant screech, you launch yourself out on the winds and fly towards the Vault of Heroes.

Dawn breaks, and shafts of coral light glint on the spears of the Kappa soldiers. They see you approaching the Vault. A wave of confusion passes through the massed throng. On the flat summit of the pyramid stand three Kappa warriors and—taller than the others, and of a chalky blue colouring rather than the dull red of his fellows—the Kappa leader himself. He is holding his intricate hands above Giru's force field, pouring his mystical energy into it in an attempt to break through to the Eye of the Dragon. And he is succeeding. The force field is starting to shimmer and fade.

There is no time to lose. You swoop down on to the summit of the Vault and resume your human form. The three warriors step forward to prevent you from reaching their leader. They attack you one at a time:

KAPPA WARRIORS   VIGOUR 15 each

Roll two dice:
score 2 to 6   You are hit; lose 3 VIGOUR
score 7 to 12   The Kappa warrior you are fighting
                  loses 3 VIGOUR

You must fight and defeat each of them in turn. If you succeed in killing all three, turn to **34**.

69

You fasten the straps of the shield around your left arm. It is light and comfortable, and you soon get the feel of it after a few practice manoeuvres. As long as you have this shield, you can use it in all future combats. Whenever the combat roll indicates that you have been hit and must take one or more wounds, roll one die; on a roll of 6 you manage to interpose the shield, and thus need deduct no VIGOUR points that Combat Round. To remind yourself, write in the ITEMS box on your Character Sheet: 'Shield—deflects a hit on a roll of 6.'

Pleased with your find, and certain that it will help you succeed in your quest, you return across the bamboo-covered courtyard to the plaza. Turn to **274**.

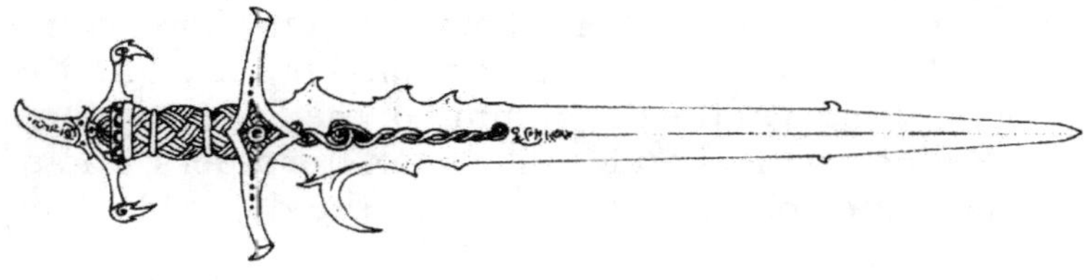

It take all your nerve, but you manage to step right up beside the astonished demon and fling the reins over his grotesque horse's head. He is half mad with fury. A vile slime flecks his lipless human jaws as he bellows his anger at you. His horse head screams and snorts and champs at the bit. He rears up to tower over you against the churning sky. Waves crash in on the shore as if in answer to his rage. One of his hoofs, chopping the air like great stone clubs, smashes against your collarbone. Lose 4 VIGOUR points.

If still alive, although sick with pain, you refuse to let go of the reins. If you draw your sword now, turn to **50**. Alternatively, you can—if you have them—use either a Wristband of Fire (turn to **9**) or a flask of fresh water (turn to **97**).

You enter a chamber which, although small, is lavishly festooned with sparkling gems, antique jewellery and piles of glistening gold coins. With many a nervous glance back at the doorway, you begin to look for items of particular interest. Lord Mantiss stands outside on the balcony, holding the stone block and bobbing his huge head approvingly.

Although he seemed to suggest you could help yourself, you decide not to take too much for fear of seeming ingracious. Will you select:

Two handfuls of gold coins?	Turn to **123**
An electrum locket?	Turn to **23**
A silver figurine with seed pearls for eyes?	Turn to **250**

You have not gone far when you come to a submerged barnacle-encrusted jetty. A small rowing boat is moored at the end of it. The jetty is under barely an inch of water, so you splash warily along it to examine the boat.

It seems to be fully seaworthy, but unfortunately there are no oars.

If you step into the boat and cast off, turn to **109**. If you return to the shore and try to think of another plan, turn to **148**.

73

You take a few purposeful strides across the lawn and stop. Something is wrong. You scan the moonlit garden with thoughts awhirl, and your gaze immediately alights on an empty pedestal. The bronze statue has moved. A shout from the mansion warns you, and you throw yourself flat on the grass just as a huge bronze fist slices through the air above your head. You look up to see the statue towering over you, grim and black against a cloudy sky. It raises its heavy armoured foot to crush you. You want to roll aside, but you find you cannot move. Fear has drained all strength from you.

A bellowing white-maned warrior charges from the darkened doorway and swings his sword against the colossus. It turns ponderously, distracted by no more than a gnat's sting—but distracted all the same. You leap to your feet as the panic-weakness leaves you. The white-haired warrior is battering furiously at the statue, though each blow breaks a fragment from his blade. 'You damned devil!' he roars. 'I'll not stand by and watch you take another life!' Even when the statue lifts its massive fists, he does not flinch. He is completely transformed now. You can no longer recognize the cringing figure whom you so despised. As the death-blow descends, his last expression is one of defiant rage.

The statue lumbers around to face you once more. Its hands are wet with blood and brains. You have seen the futility of swords against this foe. Will you retreat before it (turn to **83**) or, if you still have the spell, will you cast Burning Tiger (turn to **140**)?

74

Your sword makes an almost musical note as it leaves the scabbard. You bring it down with a heavy thunk on the side of the boat. It slices through the rope and bites deep into the wood. Feeling the rope go slack, the mermaid pouts and swims off in a huff. You see her tail rise haughtily as she plunges beneath the waves.

Turn to **131**.

75

You weave your spell with arcane words and ritual gestures, and suddenly the air is alive with an angry droning as hundreds of large hornets appear from nowhere. The four warriors are swiftly engulfed by a writhing cloud of the insects, and they duck low and try to fend off the attack as they flee. The sergeant stumbles as he runs, catching his foot on the edge of a tipped flagstone, and falls under a buzzing mass. The others run across the plaza and disappear into a ruined building. Strangely, it is only now that they begin to scream. You dispel the hornets, but it is too late to save the sergeant. He is already fatally stung. His swollen lips move feebly, as though he is trying to tell you something.

If you bend down and catch his dying words, turn to **29**. If you continue on into the city, turn to **48**.

76

Perhaps you should have washed the blood off your boots after all. That was obviously what enabled the dim-witted hemophage to track you through the maze of tunnels. You now have the more urgent problem of recovering your sword, which is stuck to a metal plate in the ceiling of the tunnel. You can reach it easily enough, but all your strength is not enough to pull it free. The plate's magnetic grip is too strong.

Magnets are rare in your world, but you have used them in some magical experiments and know that they lose their magnetism if heated. If you have not summoned it already, you could call on your Burning Tiger (turn to **30**). If that seems a waste of the spell, perhaps you have a Wristband of Fire (turn to **269**)? Failing both of these, you must abandon your sword and carry on (turn to **160**).

77

'We play this game with caltrops,' they announce, smirking. A bag of caltrops is duly produced. These are small metal items consisting of four spikes radiating from a central hub. The spikes are poisoned.

'I will drop this ball,' explains one of the gloomviles with ill-concealed mirth. 'You must snatch up as many jacks—sorry, caltrops—as you can between the first and second bounce. Then I will do the same, and the winner is the one who gets most caltrops.'

Roll one die. The number you roll represents the maximum number of caltrops you could grab if you wished to while the ball is bouncing. However, each caltrop you pick up will cost you 2 VIGOUR points (because of the poison on the spikes), so you may not wish to grab all you have time to.

After you have had your go and applied the VIGOUR loss, roll one die again. This is how many caltrops your gloomvile opponent scoops up. He is unaffected by poison.

If he beats you, turn to **267**. If you win, turn to **118**. If the game is a draw, turn to **159**.

78

Fighting to concentrate despite the blinding pain inside your skull, you manage to groan out the mystic phrases of the spell. It takes effect at once and the pain vanishes. You almost believe there is a look of frustration and amazement on the Kappa leader's inscrutable face as you kick him away.

Turn to **154**.

79

You leap up the steps behind the fleeing mynah. The chase carries you up some six storeys and at last you emerge, breathless and shaking with fury, on the windswept roof. There is a cold spray of drizzle in the air. To your horror, the mynah is perched at the very edge of the flat roof, on a weathered parapet overlooking the quadrangle. It sees you. For a moment you watch one another with what seems to be an air of mutual dislike. Then it spreads its wings. It is about to take flight, with your Orb of Illumination still in its beak! You will never reach it in time. You must use a spell. Will it be:

Befuddle?	Turn to **296**
Dagger of the Mind?	Turn to **186**

80

The light in the room becomes dimmer. Everything seems distorted, and the walls rush past you as though you were falling. You begin to understand the truth as you approach the steps to the door—each of them is a towering cliff in front of you. The black arch of the doorway seems to rise up to the very edge of heaven. You look at your hands, but see only the rasping chitinous limbs of an insect. You have been changed into a tiny beetle.

The spider drops to the floor with a disgusting plop and begins to scuttle over to you. It throws its web like a fisherman's net. Quietly and unhurriedly, it hauls in its catch.

81

You strike the tuning fork against the stone plaque and it rings with a clear, high note. The incised musical glyph glows a bright gold in response and as you watch, the door slides ponderously up into the wall. Watery emerald light filters out through a shower of dust.

You step into a humid chamber bathed in a deep green radiance. Limpets and fronds of seaweed festoon the rough stone walls, giving it the appearance of an undersea grotto. Beside a sparkling pool, a shrivelled old man sits at a table of unpolished coral. At first glance, the dim light makes it seem that he has two heads—but then you see that he actually has a huge globular spider squatting on one shoulder. A few crudely hewn steps lead down to where he is sitting. You descend these and stand watching him, trying to throw off the qualmy notion that the spider is whispering something in his ear. Suddenly the old man looks up.

'Aha!' he says in a thin reedy voice. 'I don't get many visitors. You have Mantiss's tuning fork, I see. Did you steal it from him—that charlatan, that self-styled patrician? Perhaps you slew him, eh?'

What will you reply to this outburst: that you killed Mantiss (turn to **145**) or that he gave you the tuning fork as a gift (turn to **63**)?

82

Ascending the cellar steps, you observe that your robes are stained a deep blue where they trailed in the water. You quickly guess that the Kraken must have discharged ink into the water during the dosing stages of your fight. You have known octopuses to resort to this ploy when imperilled. You can collect some of the ink if you wish, but to do this you must empty out whatever was previously in the bottle or flask you use to hold the ink. You might use your water-flask, for example, and in this case you would note down on your Character Sheet that the flask now contained Kraken ink instead of fresh water.

Whether or not you collect up any of the ink, you now leave the cellar. Turn to **107**.

83

Where will you run—out into the street (turn to **223**) or back into the mansion (turn to **4**)?

84

The room beyond the door is bathed in the flickering light of three grey candles, each as tall as you are. You can see a door in the far wall of the room. A trio of gaunt figures crouch within a pentacle chalked on the floor. Their robes spill out behind them like pools of shadow and their flesh is a bloodless grey-white. They appear to be playing a game involving a rubber ball and small metal jacks. They look around furtively, and one glance into those bleak eyes haunted with malice is enough to unnerve you. They are gloomviles. One of them addresses you in tomb-cold tones. 'Join us for a game, sorcerer.' He rattles some dice in his pallid thin hand. Will you:

Go over and join in the game?	Turn to **193**
Snuff out the candles?	Turn to **297**
Cross to the door on the other side of the room?	Turn to **163**

85

You stumble desperately along in near-darkness. Behind you, the sentinel crabs pour like a hungry black tide into the alleyway, eager to tear your fragile flesh with their hard, snapping claws. In your panic-stricken flight you blunder into the corpse of the pirate. Stumbling, you stare for a moment straight into the shadowy lines of his dead face. You regain your footing and scramble breathlessly on. The clattering sounds of pursuit stop abruptly. You glance back over your shoulder to see why, and the sight makes your stomach churn with revulsion. Chancing upon the pirate's corpse, the crabs are unable to resist the lure of carrion meat. They swarm all over the body, plucking at it ravenously. In their senseless exultation at the grisly feast they have forgotten you entirely. You hurry east to the plaza and make your way south to the Bridge of Blue Skulls.

Turn to **108**.

You begin to attune your mystic senses to the frequency you have chosen but, instead of gaining control of the Eye, you discover that it is beginning to drain the strength out of you. Your lips shape a scream, but no sound emerges. You are helpless. The Eye is draining your very essence to add to its own power. You can only return the shocked stare of the Kappa leader as you gradually fade out of existence and merge with the green glow of the Eye. You dared to tamper with forces you did not fully understand, and you have paid the ultimate price.

You lower yourself over the side of the boat, shivering as the icy water seeps through your clothes, and strike out for the western shore. Fatigued as you are after your adventures, a strong undertow soon threatens to drag you under. You struggle on and at last manage to reach a sandbank jutting out from the shoreline. You lie there in a bedraggled heap for a few moments while you get your breath back.

You now see that your backpack came open while you were in the water. You must roll for each of your items to see if you lost it. You do not need to check for your sword or (if you have them) the Orb of Illumination and the Glove of Unerring Dexterity. All your other items have a chance of being lost, however. Roll one die for each item in turn. On a roll of 1 to 4, the item is missing (cross it off your Character Sheet). On a roll of 5 or 6, you were lucky and the item is still in your possession.

After checking all your items, turn to **156**.

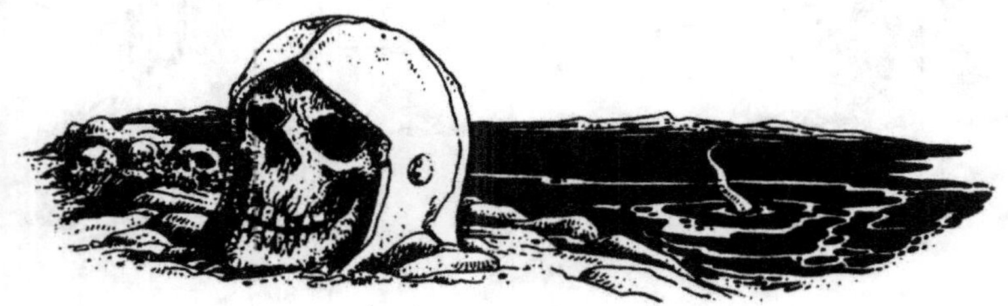

88

You return to the entrance hall. The white-haired man, still huddled and trembling on the floor, looks up with a start. He did not expect you to come back down. If you intend to explore the mansion further, will you now try the double doors (turn to **256**), or will you go down to the cellar (turn to **211**)? If you leave, turn to **299**.

89

The wind howls around the courtyard as you chant your spell. Suddenly it dies down. But in the dead calm that ensues, the howling noise still hangs in the air...

Suddenly there is a scream that makes your hair stand on end. A cackling spectral figure rises from the skeleton on the ground, extends its flickering hands like claws, and flies shrieking straight towards you. The ghastly sight strikes terror into your heart.

You have summoned a malignant ghost, and must pay the price by enduring its fright attack. Roll two dice, multiply the score by two, and compare the total to your current VIGOUR. If the number is equal to or less than your VIGOUR, you survive the ghost's fright attack; shaken, you watch as it fades away (turn to **242**). If the number is greater than your VIGOUR, however, then the terrible scare stops your heart, and your quest ends here.

90

You manage to leap on to a more stable section of the roof and sigh with relief. Treading uneasily across the remaining distance to the crystalline block, you peer into its murky depths. Within, you seem to discern the outlines of a tall robed figure. The crystal surface is cold to the touch—but not cold enough to be ice.

How long has it stood here, you wonder. How long has the faintly glimpsed figure been trapped within it? If you try and free him, turn to **201**. If you hurry back down to the ground floor and get on with your search for Master Giru, turn to **241**.

91

No sooner have you made a move towards the passage than the armoured idol stirs and rises slowly to its feet. With a clanking gait it lumbers towards you, menacing you with the swords held in each of its four hands.

You have a chance to run before it gets to you—across the courtyard and back out on to the plaza (turn to **274**). If you prefer to meet it in battle, will it be with your sword (turn to **270**) or with your sorcery (turn to **45**)?

92

Your heart sinks. Though you are trained in many unarmed combat techniques, they seem a poor match for the slashing fangs and talons of the savage hemophage.

HEMOPHAGE   VIGOUR 12

Roll two dice:
score 2 to 7   You are wounded, lose 3 VIGOUR
score 8 to 12   The hemophage loses 2 VIGOUR

Note that your kicks and punches inflict only 2 point wounds, rather than the usual 3 points. If you are wearing the Glove of Unerring Dexterity it will, of course, continue to add 1 to all your Combat Rolls.

If you kill the hemophage, turn to **76**.

93

You walk along the passage and emerge through a concealed space behind a pillar into the cavernous entrance hall. A cold sea breeze is howling around the Citadel and throwing in scattered leaves and a spray of drizzle through the open doorway.

You decide to leave and head down to the western shore. Turn to **20**.

94

The flying reptile comes swooping down, snapping at you with the sharp teeth that line its elongated maw.

Roll three dice (or roll one die three times and add the scores together). If the total is greater than your current AGILITY, turn to **136**. If the total is equal to or less than your AGILITY, turn to **249**.

95

Will you cast;

A Deadly Swarm spell?	Turn to **185**
A Mirage spell?	Turn to **169**

If you have neither of these, you must resort to using your sword (turn to **74**).

96

[Illustration on next page]

The door is of a strange metal with a purple hue. You have never seen anything like it before. Set into the middle is a tablet of rose-red stone in which a single angular glyph has been incised. You puzzle over this for a moment or two. It seems vaguely familiar. You scratch your head. Then it comes to you—the glyph represents a specific musical note, part of a tonal 'alphabet' devised by the scholars of Thalios. Some of this musical notation has survived the centuries since Thalios fell, being handed down to the present in the form of certain arcane cadences used in ritual sorcery. You are thus able to interpret the note which this glyph represents.

The door has no handle, nor does it yield to pushing. Perhaps there is some item in your backpack which would open it? You might try:

A silver figurine with pearl eyes	Turn to **246**
A jewelled harp	Turn to **16**
A tuning fork	Turn to **81**
An unidentified potion in an alabaster jar	Turn to **65**

Or, if you cannot or will not use any of these items, you can continue along the corridor (turn to **288**).

Keeping a tight grip on the reins with one hand, you hurriedly draw out the flask and uncork it with your teeth. Your hand is shaking slightly as you hold the open flask menacingly above Nuckelavee's skinless flank, but your voice is bold and resolute. 'Time to parley,' you tell him. 'I've a hunch you wouldn't enjoy it if I were to pour this over you. Why don't you just carry me across to the Consul's Palace and then we'll go our separate ways.'

'What?' he roars in his distorted, reverberating voice, flayed face black with wild fury. 'You would ride me across the Whale Road? Ride Nuckelavee, Lord of the Waves, like a common steed? I warn you, mortal—'

You allow a single drop of the water to fall from the flask. It sizzles on Nuckelavee's body like an acid. 'It is I who must warn you, Lord of the Waves,' you counter affably. 'Carry me over the water, my lord, or suffer the consequences.'

For all his blustering, the enraged demon knows you have the upper hand. At least he allows you to climb up on to his back. He leaps out across the chilling sea, cutting the waves like loam under his hard hoofs. A strange fearsome noise flies on the wind: Nuckelavee's mad and mirthless laughter. For all your revulsion, you cling tightly to his grisly torso and wait for the terrible ride to end. At last you are across the bay. Pale and uneasy, you jump down from the demon's back. He watches you with a look of seething hatred. Your hand still holds the reins.

'It is time to release me, mortal,' he mutters sinisterly. 'You must keep your part of our bargain.'

'One need not show honour to a demon,' you reply. With that, you empty the flask on to his slimy flesh.

He gives a scream of agonized outrage as the fresh water burns him. Maddened by pain, he plunges back into the cold sea and sinks beneath the waves. You shudder briefly, then turn away. Turn to **128**.

98

The air is suddenly filled with a seething mass of angrily buzzing hornets. The hemophage stares dumbfounded as the conjured insects surge over it, lashing out with their needle-sharp stings. It flails wildly in a useless attempt to fend off the attack. You laugh at the reptilian grin fixed on its long maw—it suddenly looks comical rather than bloodthirsty. Harassed and hurt, the beleaguered monster stumbles back down the passage with the droning swarm in pursuit.

Turn to **76**.

99

There are two doors off the landing. One is of a curious design—a portal of charred wood set with roughly-hewn lumps of jet. If you go through this door, turn to **84**.

If you try the other, which is of plain oak, turn to **238**.

100

A faint image rises out of the shingle close by you. It is the ghost of the beggar you met earlier. Its body is pierced by a dozen spears and there are only hollow sockets where once were its eyes. You guess that the beggar must have run into a Kappa patrol not long after he left you.

'Who is there?' moans the ghost, reaching out towards you with its moon-pale hands. 'I sense another. Help poor Boolag if you can, I beg you.'

'You are past any help that I can give,' you tell the ghost. 'I have called you here to help me. Tell me if you know of any way across to the Consul's Palace.'

'A man rowed to this shore, a pirate. I saw him moor his boat south of here. I saw him hide the oars under a thorn bush nearby. I saw this, when I still had eyes to see with.'

The ghost advances upon you, groaning, twisting its diaphanous fingers in a pleading gesture. It walks right through you, wracking your body with an uncontrollable shudder. You feel as though the blood in your veins had momentarily run with ice, and you cannot quite suppress a cry of fear. When you have recovered your composure enough to look around, the ghost is no longer there.

Turn to **220**.

101

In case there are Kappa observing the building from outside, you lace your fingers around the Orb of Illumination and use only a single narrow beam to show you the way. It would not do to have a light spotted in one of the Palace windows.

After almost half an hour of aimless searching from room to room, you are beginning to think you should go back and try the other way. At that moment, just as you are passing a mosaic screen set in one wall of the passage, you hear a scratching sound. Your first thought is of rats, and you know you are right when you see the frail mosaic wall crumbling and a hundred tiny red eyes glare at you from the yawning darkness beyond. They pour through the gap, squeaking hungrily. You catch the damp furry smell of them as you dash back along the corridor. You sweep many aside with your sword, but still more rush in. Evilly sharp teeth tear through the tough leather of your boots, lacerating your skin.

By the time you have got to the door at the end of the corridor and slammed it shut against their pursuit, you have lost 4 VIGOUR points. You now have no choice but to head back, towards the west tower. Turn to **168**.

102

The interior of the Citadel is unlit. To enter and explore it, you must still have your Orb of Illumination. If you do, turn to **225**. If you have lost the Orb, you must make your way down to the shore by turning to **20**.

103

After a long, exhausting climb you reach a chill dank room and feel the fresh night air on your face. Edging towards a window, you look out across the quadrangle. You are on the ground floor of one of the ruined buildings north of the Pantechnicon. The quadrangle is swarming with Kappa patrols, swinging the beams from their flickering green lanterns across the crumbling facades as they search for you. You shrink back into the shadows just in time. One of the lantern-beams sweeps across the front of this building. Fortunately, the Kappa seem to be gradually making their way south. In a few minutes the quadrangle should be clear and you can move on.

'Pieces of eight!'

You are startled by the sudden voice right beside you in the darkness. The mynah bird you encountered earlier jumps on to your shoulder. It is obviously attracted by the dim glow of your Orb of Illumination because, before you can react, it has seized the Orb and torn it away with its powerful beak. You emit a stifled cry of rage and snatch at it, but it evades you with a flurry of black wings and flies off up the staircase to the next floor.

If you hope to regain your magical Orb you must pursue it (turn to **79**). If you think you can manage without the Orb, turn to **241**.

104

A tiger-like creature of incandescent flame flickers into being in response to your spell. When its furibund mind realizes that there is no opponent for it to rend and sear, it greets you with a hot moody snarl and curls reluctantly around the block of dark crystal.

Within moments, as the flames lick and curl across its surface, the block begins to melt like muddy ice. The tiger fades from existence leaving only a few fragile glassy splinters. Turn to **276**.

'You rizk my dizpleazure,' says Mantiss as you back away shaking your head. Somehow he manages to inflect his buzz with a note of threat. Suddenly he throws the chunk of masonry down with an angry cry and stamps his booted foot petulantly. 'Really, thiz iz unaczeptable. Zaviour or not, I muzt teach you zome mannerz!'

With that, he whisks a slim sharp rapier from under his cloak and advances along the balcony towards you.

LORD MANTISS   VIGOUR 15

Roll two dice:

score 2 His sword-thrust finds your heart and you die instantly

score 3 to 7   You are wounded; lose 3 VIGOUR

score 8 to 12   Lord Mantiss loses 3 VIGOUR

If you *flee* by running along to the end of the balcony and down the stairs, turn to **221**. If you fight him and win, turn to **122**.

You find a thick, resinous oil in stoppered jars beside the altar stone. Once you have poured some of this into the braziers it is a simple matter to ignite them with sparks from a flint left here for the purpose. As the heat of the rekindled flames rise through vents in the ceiling, you hear a scraping noise and see a corroded grating in the wall slide up to reveal a narrow passage.

You could still leave and return to the plaza (turn to **274**) but can you resist the lure of this new route? If you explore the passage, turn to **91**.

The white-haired man ventures a nervous glance as you pass. 'You don't understand,' he whines. 'If you step outside you'll end up like Wulfric.'

You reach down angrily and grab the front of his

tunic. 'What do you suggest instead? Should I cower here all night? Should I allow the Kappa to make off with the Eye of the Dragon?'

He whimpers and you let him go. You regret losing your temper, but his cringing manner strains your patience. You turn and march out into the garden. Turn to **299**.

108

The curiously-named Bridge of Blue Skulls once spanned one of the proud canals of ancient Thalios, but as the land sank the sea gradually crept in. The bridge now links an island to the main part of the city. On a hill ahead of you, stark against the starry sky, looms the brooding Citadel of Conundrums. You glance down as you cross. The ground under the bridge is impassable sludge. At high tide the supports will be under several feet of water.

As you reach the south end of the bridge and start up the rough pathway to the Citadel, a ragged figure shambles from behind a gnarled tree. Startled, you jump back with your sword half-drawn. In the moonlight you see nothing more threatening than a filthy old beggar. He wanders up to you with palm outstretched and you can smell his rancid breath as he croaks, 'Money for a poor old man, noble friend. I expect no more than one piece of gold, though I'll not refuse more!'

If you give the beggar a gold piece, turn to **130**. If, in a mood of reckless charity, you choose to give him two gold pieces, turn to **217**. Remember to cross the cash off your Character Sheet. If you have no gold, or decide not to give any to him, you can ignore his grumbled curses and pass on up the path to the Citadel (turn to **41**).

109

The boat begins to drift across the bay. You crouch low in the bottom, not wishing to be spotted from the shore. Suddenly there is soft bubbling laughter and a green-

tressed Mermaid surfaces close by. She sweeps the sea playfully with her golden tail and throws up a shower of cold white droplets in your face. Giggling, she reaches into the boat and takes the loose end of the mooring rope before you can stop her. Putting the rope over one shapely shoulder, she starts pulling your boat out into the open sea.

You must do something quickly—but what? Will you draw your sword (turn to **74**), or cast a spell (turn to **95**)?

110

The water churns around you as the Kraken tries to enfold you in its madly writhing tentacles.

THE KRAKEN   VIGOUR 18

Roll two dice:
score 2 to 3   Turn to **125**
score 4 to 6   You suffer several blows—roll two dice
                 and deduct the total from your VIGOUR
score 7 to 12   The Kraken loses 3 VIGOUR

Its long arms would reach out to seize you long before you could get to the cellar door, but if you wish to *flee* then you could dive into the narrow tunnel you noticed earlier. If you attempt this, do not make the usual AGILITY roll but instead turn to **3**. If you fight on and slay the Kraken, turn to **271**.

111

You drain the flask of its contents and step out over the edge of the pit. To your amazement, it is as though you are supported by an invisible bridge. The experience of walking on thin air is rather enjoyable, and you are quite disappointed when the potion's effects wear off and you settle gently on the other side of the pit.

Your mood of exuberance at having outwitted the murderous statue soon changes once you emerge into the garden. The white-haired adventurer lies there, skull cracked open where the statue's fist struck him. Grim-faced, you crouch beside his body, despising yourself for having earlier despised him. After a moment's thought, you drag him inside the mansion. There is no time to give him a fitting burial. As you cross the silent lawn to leave, you ponder the nature of heroism. Does it show in a strutting contempt for those weaker than oneself—or in a willingness to face up to one's fear? Certainly the nameless adventurer died heroically and nobly. Would you meet death so well?

As you climb through the breach in the wall, you banish such morbid musings. You have no intention of meeting death—not tonight, anyway. After a last glance back, you turn your face to the Avenue of Sphinxes. Turn to **120**.

112

A magical gale whistles along the alleyway behind you. You are ready to run—but you hear no human shouts of astonishment as you had expected, merely the startled squawk of a bird.

Turn to **218**.

113

The enchanted wristband sends a gout of sizzling flame right into the monster's grinning face. Clutching its eyes, it stumbles back and escapes along the corridor. Its snarls of pain echo back to you from the darkness.

You have now expended all the power in the wristband, and cannot use it again in this adventure. Cross if off your Character Sheet and turn to **76**.

114

You can go no further. Even if you could find enough dry wood somewhere to make yourself a firebrand, you will still be faced with the monumental task of searching for Giru throughout the innumerable halls and corridors of the Palace. You settle yourself wearily on the steps and pull your robe tight around you to keep out the mournful drizzle. It is the first mission in which you have ever failed.

115

Boolag catches the gold piece you toss to him. "He don't like fresh water. Afraid of a fresh water bath, that's old Nuckelavee!' He cackles, obviously more than a little in need of a bath himself. 'Not afraid of much else, though.'

He pockets his money and scurries off into the shadows. Despite his decrepitude, he is quite nimble and stealthy; you soon lose sight of him. You continue up the path to the Citadel. Turn to **41**.

116

You race across the rubble-strewn marble floor and throw yourself into the mouth of the chute. A second crackling energy bolt misses you by inches. You careen down into darkness. From behind comes a series of deafening detonations as the Kappa blindly discharges its sceptre into the chute. You hear angry howling shouts dying away into the distance.

You have escaped, but the danger is not over yet. The slide you are on is nearly frictionless, and you have now built up considerable momentum. Light from the magical Orb of Illumination shows you the far end, rushing up to meet you at breakneck speed. Will you brace yourself for the impact (turn to **189**), or take more positive measures in the form of a spell (turn to **214**)?

117

The unstoppable warrior holds you in a vice-like grip and lifts you up as though you were a toy. Your faces are inches apart—the grim eternal countenance of the statue and the terror-contorted features of the all-too-frail human. With unhurried movements, it clamps its unyielding fingers around your neck and a black haze descends on your mind…

118

'Jackpot!' cries one. Your opponent takes a small engraved plaque of ivory from his robe, and for a moment you wonder just what it is that you have won. 'This is a ticket to the Arena,' he tells you.

'Upper circle,' adds another.

You take the ticket and thank them, then turn to leave. Turn to **208**.

119

On a whim, you reach down and snap off one of the spines from the creature's petrified mane. It reminds you of a sharp stalactite. You see nothing else of interest, so you put the stony spine in your backpack and return to the entrance hall.

Turn to **152**.

120

You push your way south against a gale that throws sharp needles of icy rain into your face. To either side, a line of carven sphinxes face one another across the avenue. Their marble bodies are palely luminous in the watery moonlight. Their chiselled faces seem grim and thoughtful. The raindrops could be tears on the stone cheeks.

'You, who are about to die—we salute you.'

The gravelly voice makes you jump. Your sword is halfway from its scabbard, but when you turn there is no one behind you. Surely not that mynah bird again. In your mind's eye, you close your fingers with relish about the miserable bird's neck.

'Sheathe your sword,' continues the rumbling voice. 'We are no danger to you.'

You stare in disbelief, for the words are spoken by one of the sphinx statues beside the avenue.

'We were the guardians of Thalios in ancient times,' intones another of the sphinxes, answering your unspoken query. 'The men of coral were enemies even then, but we are powerless now. We can only look down upon events.'

Another speaks in hollow melancholy tones, saying, 'Only a sorcerer born can hear our words. Tell us, what quest has brought you to the mouldering bones of poor, proud Thalios?'

Staring at the sad yet noble faces, you know you must reply. But will you answer truthfully about your purpose here (turn to **205**), or will you invent a different story (turn to **255**)?

121

The sight of the glowing gauntlet on your hand is rather incriminating. The old man looks at you through narrowed eyes. He does not believe your story.

Turn to **145**.

122

Your skin crawls as you approach the twitching insectile corpse, now leaking a turquoise ichor from several wounds. You leave the rapier—not your kind of weapon at all!—but divest Mantiss of his glowing silver gauntlet and a small steel tuning-fork that dangled on a thread around his segmented neck.

If you put on the gauntlet, turn to **236**. If not, you place the items in your backpack and descend to the ground floor of the building (turn to **241**).

123

'Thiz iz zheer greed!' cries out Mantiss in a tone of shocked disgust as you merrily stuff the coins into your backpack. You are about to protest that you only did as he suggested, but he goes on: 'Vile mizcreant! You would rob from poor truzting Mantizz, eh? You dezerve to die for your greed—but you did perform zome zmall zervize in freeing me, zo I zhall be lenient. I zhall merely leave you here for a zentury or two, giving you time to reflect on the fruitz of av arize and greed.'

Without another word, he slides the huge stone block back into place across the doorway—sealing you in! You yell and pound on the block to no avail. The mad insect-man has gone, leaving you to suffer a slow death by starvation. Your adventure is at an end.

124

Your spell creates the image of a fearsome Hydra rearing its nine heads out of a shadowy corner of the hall. Its hissing mouths drip a very convincing venomous spittle, and the two Kappa quickly forget all about you as they turn to defend themselves from this new threat.

Taking advantage of the diversion, you leap into the chute and career down into darkness. You are on a frictionless slide, and building up speed alarmingly. The end of the chute is coming up fast. Will you protect yourself with a spell (turn to **214**), or just brace yourself for the impact (turn to **189**)?

125

The Kraken encircles you with its rubbery tentacles and begins to exert a bone-crushing grip. You are powerless to break free. It will gorge itself upon your mangled remains before retreating to its submerged grotto to sleep once more.

126

Only one of your opponents still stands. His eyes are blank and his face expressionless. He does not even seem to hear you when you offer him the chance to surrender. He fights on mindlessly, though the flagstones of the plaza are scarlet with his comrades' blood.

Roll two dice:
score 2 to 3   You are hit and lose 3 VIGOUR
score 4 to 12   Your opponent loses 3 VIGOUR

If you win, turn to **305**.

127

You push the wooden leg towards the hemophage, but it weaves away and you miss by a few inches. Its open jaws are poised around your wrist. Time seems to stand still; in this frozen moment, you could almost count each gleaming tooth in its wide crocodilian maw—

You scream as the hemophage's bite severs your hand! In disbelief, you watch your lifeblood spouting furiously from the torn stump. The monster only grins widely, enjoying its bloodbath. You can do nothing to staunch the bleeding. Your legs buckle and you fall to the gore-spattered floor. Life floods from you while the hemophage waits to feast.

128

Silent and stealthy, you creep along the outer wall of the Palace and into the courtyard. The ancient buildings tower up on all sides. An ornamental fountain, choked with moss and rainwater, stands in the centre of the courtyard. The statue above it has crumbled away, though some of the long-dead sculptor's genius is still there to be glimpsed in the weathered lines.

Wary in case there are Kappa soldiers about, you move out of sight into the deep shadows opposite the gate. You literally stumble upon a broken skeleton half-buried in the wet gravel. A few fragments of rusted armour still enclose it like tenacious, grasping fingers.

An adventurer who came here before you. Perhaps decades before.

You must find Master Giru, and you sense he is somewhere in the Palace. To explore it, you will need your Orb of Illumination. If you still have this item, turn to **62**. If you have lost it, turn to **114**.

129

What will you cast:

Your Deadly Swarm spell?   Turn to **298**
Your Mirage spell?   Turn to **150**

If you do not use either of these, turn to **110**.

130

He snatches the coin away and, turning a resentful scowl upon you, murmurs ungratefully as he scurries away. You doubt if you will show quite the same generosity to the next beggar you meet. You continue on towards the Citadel. Turn to **41**.

131

You have got rid of the Mermaid all right, but now you note with alarm that your boat has been snatched by a current that is taking it gradually south, out to sea. You have no choice but to swim for it.

Turn to **87**.

132

You are at the top of a short flight of steps leading down into a long hall. A feverish red light is provided by the crackling fires of three braziers that hang from the ceiling. The air holds a supernatural menace. You cannot see the floor of the hall, for it is submerged in a pool of inky darkness. At the far end, another flight of steps emerges from the darkness. The steps lead up to an alcove where a large bowl of pale shell rests on a marble stand.

If you descend into the dark and make your way along the hall, turn to **27**. If you go out and carry on along the passage, turn to **247**.

133

You drag the splintered bodies to one side of the quadrangle and conceal them in a ruined building where further patrols will not stumble across them. There is a murderous glint in your eye as you look around for the mynah. Your thoughts of savoured revenge must go unrealized for the moment—after betraying you to the two Kappa, the treacherous bird took refuge somewhere in the ruins.

Turn to **54**.

134

With the plank gone, you have no way of getting over the pit. It is too wide to jump. Sorrowfully, you realize that although you have outwitted the deadly statue, you are now trapped in this crumbling mansion. There is no way out. You sit miserably on the edge of the pit. Now you can only watch the slimy water flow past below and wait for a Kappa patrol to find you. You have exchanged a quick death for a slow and painful one.

135

'Wulfric!' howls the white-haired adventurer. 'It got him. I couldn't have done anything. What could I do? It would've got me too if I'd crossed that threshold into the garden. We're trapped in here, I tell you! O gods, gods!' He rakes at his hair and gibbers until you none-too-kindly snarl at him to shut up.

Ahead of you lies a wide pit spanned by a single narrow plank. You discover that the pit opens on to a sluggish underground stream some distance below. Several spikes of rusty iron thrust up from the black water, making the prospect of crossing the plank somewhat daunting.

If you chance it anyway (and for this you must have a current AGILITY of at least 4—anything less and you would certainly fall), turn to **17**. If you return to the entrance hall, turn to **152**.

136

You yell in agony as the monster tears a long gash in your side. Lose 7 VIGOUR points. If you are still alive, turn to **66**.

137

As if guided by a sixth sense, you suddenly remember the mysterious potion. You are not one to disregard a hunch—you unstopper the jar and, gulp back the contents. It has a sweet, syrupy taste, and as you feel your muscles swelling you realize you have just drunk a Potion of Strength. Your biceps are like steel bands.

You take hold of the grating and wrench at the bars. They buckle like tissue paper, allowing you to step through and take the black reins. As the effect of the potion wears off, you leave the room and make your way down the passage opposite. Turn to **93**.

138

Steeling yourself, you try to thrust the wooden pegleg right into the snapping jaws of the monster. Your only hope is to wedge its deadly maw open.

Roll one die. Add 1 to the number rolled if you are wearing the Glove of Unerring Dexterity. If you score 1 to 3, turn to **127**. If you score 4 or more, turn to **251**.

139

The Deadly Swarm is an excellent spell to use against a human foe, but it is totally useless against the lumbering idol. The buzzing insects cluster angrily around the idol as it advances towards you, but their stings cannot penetrate the heavy armour plates.

You must fight. Turn to **270**.

140

It is the first time you have even seen the savage tiger of flame reluctant to tackle a foe. Nonetheless, it slinks forward and leaps upon the statue as you command. The fiery claws have some effect on the bronze body of the statue—but not enough, and you quickly see that the tiger is bound to lose this battle.

You hurry south along the Avenue of Sphinxes. Turn to **28**.

141

There is a noise like a thunderclap. A hissing blue bolt of energy lances past your head and throws a shower of molten stone fragments from the wall. You drop low as you turn. Two Kappa stand in the doorway. One of them holds a strange steel sceptre, and the glowing tip of this is pointing straight at you. You have three options:

Cast a spell	Turn to **302**
Fight	Turn to **229**
Escape by diving into the chute in the wall	Turn to **116**

142

You fall to your knees in the mire. Your limbs quake with exhaustion and you are almost sobbing for breath. Blood streams from a deep gash on your brow. Through a red haze you stare at the armoured bodies of the fallen undead. For a few moments while locked in mortal combat with them, you almost gave in to despair. But you prevailed—just as you will prevail against the hated Kappa, by your oath as a Warrior Mage of the Elder Realm. You pick yourself up and struggle the rest of the way to the shore.

Turn to **128**.

143

You are a little over halfway across the pit when you begin to lose your balance. Teetering precariously, arms flailing like windmills, you gape for a horror-struck moment at the churning water below. Then you make a desperate leap for the edge.

Try to score less than or equal to your current AGILITY on two dice. If you succeed, you land—shaken but safe—on the far side of the pit (turn to **52**). If you fail, you topple over into the pit and fall to your death on the iron spikes.

144

You step out of the alley into a large quadrangle dominated by the ruins of a huge domed building—the Amber Pantechnicon. Around the perimeter of the quadrangle, the cobblestones are littered with broken tiles which have fallen from the crumbling roofs. About fifty metres away, their thin coral bodies gleaming darkly in the moonlight, two Kappa are patrolling the quadrangle. They begin to move in your direction, and you quickly hide in the shadows. They come to a halt in front of the gated archway of the Pantechnicon and begin to consult a plaque that one of them carries at its belt. Occasionally you hear them exchanging words in their strange fluting speech.

It occurs to you that the plaque may be a map of some sort—a sea-dwelling species like the Kappa are hardly likely to use paper, after all. Perhaps they are discussing which part of the city to patrol next. One option is to edge around the quadrangle away from them and head south along the Avenue of Sphinxes (turn to **304**). Otherwise, you could wait where you are until the Kappa move on (turn to **170**).

145

'My good friend Mantiss!' he howls. 'Murdered by a young upstart who presumes to wear a wizard's robe. Chu's friend will show you the power of a true sorcerer, you atrocious assassin. I doubt whether you will survive the demonstration.'

He cackles and glances expectantly at the spider on his shoulder. Its myriad eyes are beginning to shine with a sinister light. You must quickly decide whether to hit it with your sword (turn to **188**) or run for the door (turn to **67**).

146

Still stunned by the fall, your reactions are too slow. The enormous weight of the pillar smashes down on to your squirming body, crushing the life from you as an apothecary might grind a tiny beetle in his pestle and mortar. Your adventure ends here.

147

Several Kappa warriors are crossing the quadrangle. You hide under a ramshackle portico, but they seem too absorbed to notice you in any case. They are dragging something limp behind them—something which their huge pet sentinel crabs are ripping at hungrily. Moonlight falls on a dead white face as they emerge from the shadows of the Pantechnicon. You hope fervently that it is not the body of Master Giru. At last the Kappa leave the quadrangle, hauling their grisly burden with them, and you slip out from the portico.

Turn to **54**.

148

If you have them, you might use either a Séance spell (turn to **281**) or a Potion of Wind Walking (turn to **25**).

If you have neither of these, or think they would not be of any use here, you must go to the boat and cast off (turn to **109**).

149

There is a screech of tortured metal from your sword as the ebon blade snaps in two. For the remainder of the adventure (until and unless you can get the sword repaired) you must reduce all Combat Rolls by 1—eg, if you rolled a 6 in combat you would count it as a 5.

Not without bitterness, you observe that the crystalline block remains unscratched. If you still want to free the trapped figure, you might have more success with your Burning Tiger spell. If you have not yet used this spell, and want to cast it now, turn to **104**. More probably you will choose to return to the ground floor and go on your way—in which case turn to **241**.

150

You use the spell to fashion an illusory copy of yourself. The Kraken blinks its hideous eyes as it tries to distinguish the two.

Roll one die. If you roll a 1, 2 or 3 then the Kraken attacks your illusory duplicate, giving you time to race up the cellar steps to safety: turn to **107**. If you roll a 4 or higher then the Kraken disregards your illusion and attacks the real you: turn to **110**.

151

You realize with dismay that you can call none of your spells to mind. The presence of the arch-demon Nuckelavee has neutralized your magical powers. Hopefully this is only a temporary effect—though, unless you find a way to beat him, that will hardly matter anyway. One of his huge pale hoofs smashes against your arm, sending waves of pain through your whole body. Lose 4 VIGOUR points and, if you are still alive, quickly make up your mind what to do next.

Will you attack Nuckelavee with your sword (turn to **50**), or will you try using one of your items (turn to **7**)?

152

The adventurer looks up as you pass and whines, saying, 'You don't understand. If you step outside you'll end up like Wulfric.'

'What do you propose I do? Should I cower here all night while the Kappa execute their nefarious plans?'

You consider taking him with you on the principle
that two swords are better than one, but you know he
would be of no use. His spirit is broken. You regret
losing your temper with the poor man, but you can think
of nothing to say to him. You shake your head and
march out into the garden without a backward glance.

Turn to **73**.

153

Your opponent flies around you and cuts off your escape
when you are only halfway across the plank. It circles
around you to prevent you from retreating. You must
now fight it while trying desperately to maintain your
precarious balance.

Roll two dice:

score 2 to 7   You are hit and lose 3 VIGOUR
score 8 to 12   The prosopteryx loses 3 VIGOUR

Every Combat Round, in addition to the usual Combat
Roll, you must check to see whether you lose your
footing on the narrow plank. You do this by rolling one
die; if the score is equal to or less than your current
AGILITY then you are okay for that Combat Round, but
if you roll more than your current AGILITY then you fall
into the black pit and are impaled on the metal spikes
below.

If you manage to stay on the plank and defeat the
prosopteryx, turn to **222**.

154

You reach out for the casket. It is of a dark burnished
metal that gleams fierily in the dawn light. The hasp is
incised with a runic symbol. As soon as you touch this,
the lid flies open and your face is bathed in the golden-
green light of the huge gemstone within. It is smooth
and clear, as green as the sea. The Eye of the Dragon.

You are holding your breath as your hand closes
around it. Immediately you sense dozens of psychic

frequencies radiating from it, entering your mind. All but one of the frequencies are magical traps. They will scramble your brain if you do not filter them out. The last frequency is the correct one—the frequency to which you must attune your mind in order to control the Eye. Within seconds you have analysed the frequencies and filtered out all but three. One of these three will enable you to harness the power of the Eye, while the other two will destroy you if you try to tune in to them. Only a skilled sorcerer could have narrowed the field this much. Only a master sorcerer could make the final, fateful decision. Which will you choose:

The highest frequency?	Turn to **248**
The intermediate frequency?	Turn to **86**
The lowest frequency?	Turn to **175**

155

Standing once more on the steps above the region of shadow, you drink the contents of the jar. Immediately you feel weightless, and you are able to cross the hall safely by walking on thin air. You know that the potion's effect does not last long, so you snatch up the contents of the bowl as soon as you reach it and then return hastily to the exit before examining your find. The darkness hangs beneath you. You sense the frustrated malignance of the spirits within it. The potion wears off just as you reach the safety of the passage, and you settle gently to the hard stone floor.

The item you have acquired is a large sheet of strange white fabric. Although very tough, it is tissue-thin and folds into a small wad which you place in your backpack. This done, you make your way back to the ground floor. Turn to **88**.

156

You slowly trudge along the sandbank. The ground underfoot is a waterlogged quagmire in which you sink almost to the level of your knees. It sucks you down and

seems to begrudge your every step with a sound like the hideous smacking of giant lips. Clinging weeds slow your progress and you are soon feeling weary. The shore is barely twenty metres off, but it seems ten times that distance.

Two tall figures rise up from the mud to block your path. A cloud drifts across the moon, and you see them only faintly—dark and deadly figures in clanking armour. Slimy tendrils of seaweed hang from their rusty antique swords and barnacles crust the ornate iron plates that cover them. There is a rotting stench, barely masked by the smell of the sea. A shaft of moonlight falls across their open visors, and all you see within are the fleshless weed-draped grins of skulls. They are lich knights, drowned warriors from ancient times who exist only to bring death to others. There is no time even to think of a spell as they lift their huge two-handed swords—nor can you *flee* from them with the marshy sand tugging at your ankles. You must fight for your life.

| First LICH KNIGHT | VIGOUR 15 |
| Second LICH KNIGHT | VIGOUR 15 |

Roll two dice:

score 2 to 4	You are hit twice; lose 6 VIGOUR
score 5 to 7	You are hit once; lose 3 VIGOUR
score 8 to 12	One of the lich knights (you choose) loses 3 VIGOUR

If you overcome one of them, turn to **11**.

157

As you cast your spell there is a roar of rushing flame and a tiger of flickering fire erupts from one of the braziers. It pounces upon the back of the advancing idol and a titanic battle is joined. The idol slashes with its swords in a blur of motion, but the tiger is a powerful adversary and hangs on savagely to its foe. Its raking claws cast rivulets of molten silver from the idol's armour.

If you wish to wait to see the outcome of the battle,

turn to **224**. If you have given up your intention of investigating the side passage, you can now return to the plaza outside by turning to **274**.

158

You blunder straight into a host of the murderous monsters. Hard snapping claws rip your clothing, tear bloody chunks from your flesh. You scream once, and the shrill cry echoes back unheeded from the empty buildings as the crabs swarm over you. They are a ravenous black tide, with no thought but to glut themselves on your torn flesh. Your adventure has come to a sticky end.

159

'A commendable attempt,' acknowledges your opponent. 'As a consolation prize, allow me to present you with a fine quill pen.' He produces the item from his sable robe and hands it to you.

They ask you to join them within the pentacle, but you nervously explain that you have to hurry along.

Turn to **208**.

160

You are not at all happy about leaving your trusty sword behind, but you are resourceful and will manage without it. At the end of the tunnel you find a room piled high with old bones, all doubtless picked clean by the gluttonous hemophage. You are glad to see that the stupid monster also left some of the weapons and armour of its victims here. You try out some of the weapons for balance, and finally select a strong broadsword to take with you. It is not as fine a sword as the one you lost, however, so for the rest of the adventure you must subtract 1 from every Combat Roll you make. (If, for example, you were to roll a 6 then this would actually count as a 5. A roll of 2 is unchanged.) Should you be wearing the Glove of Unerring Dexterity, its bonus will of course cancel out the penalty due to your new weapon.

A corridor leads on from the room. You proceed along it. Turn to **219**.

161

The old man seems to find your story plausible. He smiles and tells you his name is Chu. He does not introduce you to his spider. Since you wear the gown of a sorcerer, Chu offers to show you a conjuring trick. A copper wristband jangles on his scrawny arm as he places three shiny turret shells on the table. Beside them he puts a large pearl.

'I will put the pearl under one of the shells—like so. You must watch carefully as I switch the shells about. Try to keep your eye on the one with the pearl. Easy, eh? Let's make the trick more entertaining—you wager one of your possessions against one of mine.'

If you are not willing to stake one of your items on such a trick, leave the room and turn to **288**. If you accept Chu's offer, decide which item you are going to wager (it cannot be your sword or the Orb of Illumination) and turn to **6**.

162

A slight draught along the passage wafts a charnel odour in your face. You soon discover the source of the smell as the passage widens out into a fetid room where the walls and floor are sticky with half-dried blood. It is like a slaughterhouse, though you see no carcasses lying about. Feeling your gorge rise at the awful stench and sight of the place, you pinch your nostrils and hasten over to one of several exits. You find yourself in a confusing maze of tunnels, but your sense of direction is good and you are confident of finding your way through them.

You notice with some disgust that your boots are soaked in blood, causing you to leave a trail of gory footprints as you progress through the winding tunnels. If you want to clean your boots, you could wash off the blood with the water in your flask—or with something else, if you have any other liquids. If you do this, cross the liquid you use from your Character Sheet and turn to **308**. If you decide not to bother, turn to **252**.

163

They come to the very edge of the pentacle. It seems that an invisible barrier keeps them confined within it. 'Wait!' they cry in unison as you reach the far door. 'You don't have to enter the pentacle. Just come to the edge for one game.'

If you do as they suggest, turn to **42**. If you hurry on your way, turn to **208**.

164

Roll two dice. If the score is equal to or less than your current AGILITY, turn to **166**. If the number you roll is greater than your AGILITY, turn to **146**.

165

A short unpleasant laugh cuts through the night as you drop all your gold pieces. Remember to cross them off your Character Sheet.

'Be off with you!' snaps the shrill voice of another unseen waylayer.

With at least two armed assailants behind you, you have no choice but to comply. You hasten along to the far end of the alleyway without looking back. Suddenly there is a rush of air past your cheek and a mynah bird flies by, chortling. Realizing you have been fooled you turn around, but it is too dark in the alley to search for your money. You decide to continue. Turn to **144**.

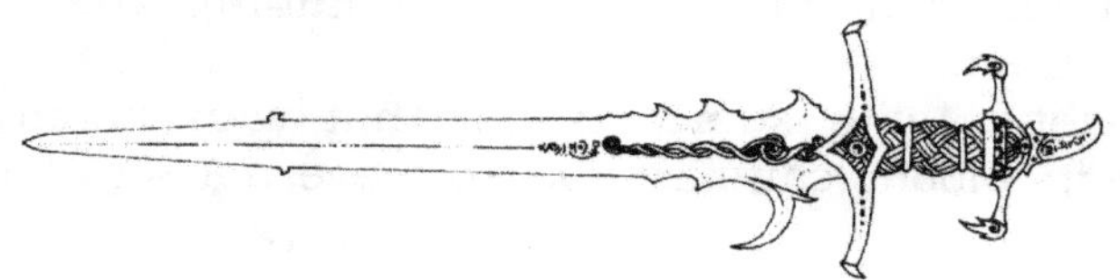

166

You throw yourself to one side just in time. The enormous weight of crumbling rock smashes down beside you, causing a web of hairline cracks to spread across the marble floor. More chunks of rubble drop from the ceiling to fall all around you, and you fold your arms over your head until the barrage subsides.

Slowly you clamber to your feet. Staring at the vast toppled pillar, you are hardly able to believe your lucky escape. Moonlight slants in through the broken roof, and in its pallid glimmer you see a staircase leading down. Slowly you make your way down to the ground floor. Turn to **241**.

167

You pull the cork from the bottle and cast its contents over the surface of the crystalline block. If you had hoped to see the mysterious substance fume and dissolve away, you are disappointed. You cast the empty bottle aside. You are fairly confident, at least, that the vinegar would not have been of any use to you.

If you now abandon the block and go downstairs, turn to **241**. If you still want to free the trapped figure, you can use a jewelled harp (turn to **195**), a Burning Tiger spell (turn to **104**) or a blow from your sword (turn to **149**).

168

Your fruitless search takes you through scores of forlorn empty rooms and twisting corridors. Finding a grand staircase, you ascend to the upper apartments of the west tower.

A startling sight awaits you—a disembodied yellow hand which is floating towards you through the air! When it sees (?) you, it splays its fingers in mimed surprise and then begins to drift away along the passage, beckoning you to follow. It leads you through a series of echoing corridors and hallways and up several flights of stairs before finally coming to a halt in front of

a sturdy bronze door. An impatient jerk of its thumb indicates that it wants you to go through.

If you open the door, turn to **228**. If you use an ESP spell first to find out what is on the other side, turn to **194**.

169

Your spell creates the image of a handsome merman in the water some distance away. The mermaid stares at it in fascinated astonishment. You concentrate and cause the image to smile and turn away. She faithlessly deserts you and plunges through the waves in pursuit of your enticing illusion. You chuckle, hoping the beautiful creature will not be too distraught when she discovers she has been duped.

Turn to **131**.

170

The Kappa eventually come to a decision and head, off southwards. Alert for other patrols, you creep swiftly across the quadrangle to the shadowy bulk of the Pantechnicon. Valuable artifacts of many kinds—some of them, perhaps, magical—were once stored within this colossal edifice. No such treasures are visible when you peer between the bars of the huge gate—just the inky blackness of the building's interior. A lone albatross gives a mournful cry as it wheels in the night sky. You pause for only a moment, then seize the gate and haul it open. The shriek of rusted hinges echoes back loudly from the buildings enclosing the quadrangle. Alarmed that you may have been heard by Kappa in the nearby streets, you hasten inside.

Turn to **192**.

171

The passage opens out into a small room. There are two alabaster jars on a cracked marble shelf. You unstopper them and sniff at the contents, readily identifying the first as a Potion of Wind Walking. You have no idea what the other might be.

You carefully place the jars in your backpack and then retrace your steps. Turn to **88**.

172

The sharp spine is unwieldy, but better than no weapon at all.

HEMOPHAGE   VIGOUR 12

Roll two dice:
score 2 to 7   You are wounded; lose 3 VIGOUR
score 8 to 12   The hemophage loses 3 VIGOUR

If you have the Glove of Unerring Dexterity it will continue to add 1 to every Combat Roll, of course. Should you win, turn to **76**.

173

You cast your spell right into the face of the hellish monster. The malicious red eyes swivel inwards as if trying to focus on several things at once. Wildly swinging its great leathery wings, the flying reptile tries to pull up. It succeeds only in tilting out of its gliding position and crashing to the Arena floor. You draw your sword and run to attack it while it is still dazed. Turn to **49**.

174

It is not especially hard to befuddle a hemophage—these creatures are hardly noted for their intelligence. It staggers to a halt as your spell takes effect. After staring around blankly as though it has forgotten what it came here for, the hemophage turns and lumbers back to its lair. You wipe a trickle of sweat from your forehead.

Turn to **76**.

175

You attune your mystic senses to the frequency you have chosen. Power flows from the Eye and courses through your body. An eerily shrieking horde of Kappa soldiers is clambering up the steps of the pyramid towards you. You watch them coolly for a moment, then slowly raise the Eye. Suddenly, a spray of searing gold-white beams flash from the sparkling gem. The Kappa halt, aghast. Every one of their swords and spears has been vaporized in that single instant.

The Kappa leader lurches to his feet. You know that he has abandoned any thought of attacking you. The Eye of the Dragon lets you see right into his mind, and you read only awe and fear there. You speak to him, and to all the Kappa, through the telepathic power of the Eye: 'You are weaponless, defeated. Return to your own realm. Tell your people we humans have the Eye of the Dragon. If you ever attack again, be certain that we shall unleash its full force against you. Now go.'

You watch as the Kappa turn and shuffle south, out to sea. The waves close over their heads. The Kappa leader is the last to go. As he enters the water, he glances back towards you. The Eye picks up his thoughts and translates them: 'Farewell, human. You were a worthy adversary.'

You reply with a grim smile as he wades off into the surging sea. Turn to **310**.

176

The shadows issue through the archway in pursuit of you, a black tide of malice bent on your destruction. As each shadow passes through, it begins to take on form and substance. In place of shadows, you find yourself surrounded by twenty armoured gladiators with nets and tridents. You grit your teeth. You are too heavily outnumbered to stand a chance, but you refuse to die without a fight. You swing your sword in a deadly arc and leap at the nearest gladiator. To your amazement, he dissolves in a many-coloured mist the moment your blade strikes home. You sweep your sword back and another vanishes. Puffing up your cheeks, you blow at a third; he goes out like a candle flame. You were about to give up hope in the face of a horde of illusions! Laughing, you dispel the remaining gladiators with similar ease and continue further into the Citadel of Conundrums.

Turn to **162**.

177

You leap out off the twisting stairway. The high pillared walls of the vast room rush past at hair-raising speed. You land with a hideous impact that jars every bone in your body. Roll two dice—the total is the number of VIGOUR points you lose for the fall. Also deduct 1 point of AGILITY for spraining your ankle.

If you are still alive, you slope painfully from the room as, high above, Mantiss administers the *coup de grace* to your tiger. You descend to the ground floor of the building. Turn to **241**.

178

Despite a sense of unease, as though you are being watched, you cross the Arena safely and walk along the other tunnel. Outside, the streets are deserted. The Kappa patrols must all be looking for you around the Avenue of Sphinxes. Turn to **240**.

179

What plan will you try:

Drink a Potion of Wind Walking?	Turn to **25**
Play a jewelled harp?	Turn to **204**
Cast a Séance spell?	Turn to **281**

If none of these options is open to you, you must go looking for a boat: turn to **72**.

180

You stare down, awestruck, at the bay rushing past far below. Ahead lies a colossal pyramid of ochre stone: the Vault of Heroes. Kappa throng its base like ants, and

you can see the sunlight glinting on their serried spears.

'Help me steer this contraption,' calls Giru over the buffeting wind.

You look round. The two guards are gripping the rail with white fingers and look decidedly sick, but old Giru seems to be enjoying himself tremendously. 'Do you know how to steer it?' you ask him.

'No idea, but we'd better learn quickly.'

You lose no time in trimming the sail to bring your bearing directly on to the Vault. You begin to drop lower in the sky, and you can now make out four shapes on the flat summit of the Vault. Three of them are just Kappa warriors, but the fourth—even taller than the others, and robed in magnificent finery—is the Kappa leader himself. His angular fretwork hands are poised above Giru's force field, assailing it with crackling beams of pure mystic force.

'The force field I set up around the Eye,' breathes Giru in disbelief. 'He's actually breaking through it.'

Giru calls to the guards to reduce sail. They do so clumsily, causing the ship to start a rapid descent. The Kappa at the base of the pyramid see you now, and a fluting wail goes up. You are dropping right towards the summit. It is too late to pull out of the dive; you cling to the mast and brace yourselves for a crash landing. The impact splinters the ship's timbers, but none of you is badly hurt. The two guards recover immediately and leap from the wreckage to attack the Kappa leader's three warriors. Even Giru pulls a mace from his belt and lays about him with gusto. It is left to you to deal with the Kappa leader. Turn to **34**.

181

In a shower of tiles and broken stone slabs, you plunge through the collapsing roof. Before you can even draw breath to cry out, a jutting stone beam strikes your head a glancing blow. Dazed, you fall to the floor below like a rag doll. Lose 4 VIGOUR points.

If you are still alive, you gradually come to your senses. There is an ominous creak, and you stare up in horror as you behold one of the huge pillars of the room into which you have fallen beginning to topple on its heavy base. Only quick thinking might save your life. Will you:

Try to roll out of the way?	Turn to **164**
Cast a Gust of Wind Spell?	Turn to **275**
Cast an Invulnerability spell?	Turn to **215**

182

The remaining two warriors continue to attack you. With their stiff movements and grimly cast features they look more like malevolent mannikins than living men.

Roll two dice:

score 2 to 3	You are hit twice and lose 6 VIGOUR
score 4 to 5	You are hit once and lose 3 VIGOUR
score 6 to 12	One of the warriors (you decide which) loses 3 VIGOUR

If you manage to kill one of them, turn to **126**.

183

You walk south along the beach, looking for some way to get across to the Consul's Palace. You have not gone far when you come to a sunken jetty. A small rowing boat is moored at the end of it, bobbing about in the low waves. The jetty is under barely an inch of water, so you walk along it to examine the boat. It is in fine condition, but there are no oars. Still, you have no other means of getting across the bay. You climb into the boat and cast off. Turn to **109**.

184

Your sharp reflexes save you and you weave nimbly aside as the bolt streaks past and turns the floor behind you to magma. You snarl and leap towards the astonished Kappa. Turn to **39**.

185

She shrieks prettily and dives beneath the waves to avoid the threatening cloud of furiously droning insects. They hover over the water until the spell expires and they vanish, but she has been thoroughly scared off and makes no attempt to resurface.

Turn to **131**.

186

There is a startled, strangled croak as your dagger impales the wretched bird. It topples back on to the roof, a dishevelled mass of blood-stained feathers, and you run over to see what has happened to your Orb.

Turn to **306**.

187

Assailed by awful terrors beyond the bounds of reality, your tortured mind takes refuge in madness. As you stagger back out of the zone of darkness, a ghastly gibbering echoes around the hall. It is the sound of your own crazed laughter. Staggering into the passage, you seize the hoary skeleton and caper with it in a *danse macabre*. You are condemned now to the perpetual waking nightmare of insanity.

188

You draw your black sword. Will you swing it at the old man (turn to **213**), or at the spider on his shoulder (turn to **199**)?

189

You curl up as you emerge from the chute, folding your head under your arms. You hit the hard floor with sickening impact. Roll two dice and deduct the total from your current VIGOUR. If you are still alive, you roll to a painful halt against the wall. Wincing at every movement, you slowly stretch your bruised limbs and stagger to your feet. Turn to **38**.

190

Your conjured gale slams into the startled creature's back, knocking it to the ground as though it had been swatted by a giant's fist. It hisses and struggles to rise, but you draw your sword and rush in before it has a chance to take to the air once more.

Turn to **49**.

191

A vortex of flame forms in the air between you and the coldly grinning monster. In the next instant, the licking tongues of flame have coalesced into the shape of a huge tiger. It leaps upon the hemophage and presses its hot claws into sizzling flesh. The hemophage gives vent to an anguished cry and falls back. Its futile struggles continue for a few moments and then it is still. The tiger turns a flickering glare upon you as its flames die and it fades away.

Turn to **76**.

192

You walk slowly across the main hallway of the Pantechnicon. There are many niches in the side walls, built to house priceless relics. Few remain, the rest having been lost in the mad looting that took place after the fall of Thalios. A cold breeze whistles in through large gaping windows. Passing what appears to be the mouth of a chute in the wall to your right, you arrive at the end of the hallway. In an alcove here, a jewelled harp

hangs by a single thread of gold. You reach for it, mesmerized by avarice. You can sense its sorcerous power. But there is a sheet of glass across the front of the alcove. Looking more closely, you see that the bottom of the alcove slopes down into the room, and there is a gap at the bottom of the sheet of glass. If only you could break the gold thread, the harp would drop and slide under the glass into your waiting hands.

You glance nervously through the window. There are no more Kappa patrols to be seen yet, but you must not linger here overlong. If you want the harp, you must quickly think of a way to get it. Will you cast one of your spells (turn to **293**), or will you see if you can break the glass (turn to **265**)? If you decide to turn away without the harp, turn to **141**.

193

The gloomviles jump up gleefully as you cross the boundary of their pentacle. 'We play a rough game...' says one. '...Known as blackjacks,' adds another. Suddenly a knobbly fist crashes into the back of your neck and you drop to the floor. You lie stunned and helpless while their heartless smiles drift closer through the haze of gathering red darkness. Cold fingers encircle your throat. Your adventure is at an end.

194

Your spell detects human thoughts on the other side of the door. There are three men in the room. The hand gives you an 'OK' sign as you fling the door open.

Turn to **228**.

195

The first harp string that you pluck causes a ringing note to start up within the block of crystal. You are about to play on, but the note is getting louder and louder and you can see that the edges of the block are blurred by vibration. Covering your ears against the deafening whine, you throw yourself flat just as the block explodes into a thousand glassy fragments. You hear them whistle like a volley of razor-tipped arrows over your head, but none hits you. With the echo of the note still ringing in your ears, you get up and look around.

Turn to **276**.

196

The other three warriors press their ferocious attack, barely noticing as their companion falls to your killing blow.

Roll two dice:

score 2 to 3	You are hit three times—lose 9 VIGOUR
score 4 to 5	You are hit twice—lose 6 VIGOUR
score 6	You are hit once—lose 3 VIGOUR
score 7 to 12	One of your opponents (your choice) loses 3 VIGOUR

If you defeat another, turn to **182**.

197

A sudden rush of wind blows the leaping insect-man off course. He misses the staircase and goes plummeting down to the floor of the hall. He lands with a satisfying crunch and you race quickly down the stairs. He is moaning horribly, trying to drag his broken body over to where his sword lies. You heft your sword and strike off his head without compunction.

Turn to **122**.

198

Giru holds up the bottle. 'An interesting acquisition. From these symbols etched into the glass, I'd hazard a guess that you found it in the Citadel of Conundrums. Am I right? We can rig it with this sheet.'

For the first time, you notice that the model boat has no sail. 'It seems rather small for that,' you point out drily.

'Not at all. This ship is a magical item. Once the seal on the bottle is broken, it will grow to full size. As for the sheet, that's a heliacal sail which—but let me show you. Come along.'

The four of you climb the stairs and emerge on to the flat roof of the tower. Night is just a blue-grey shadow retreating westwards, and the eastern sky is beginning to show a rim of pale gold. Giru smashes the bottle against the parapet and, as he said would happen, the ship miraculously enlarges until it is some four metres long. Though he has no sorcerous powers of his own, you are learning to respect the wisdom and knowledge of the old scholar. You all climb into the ship and, at Giru's instructions, the two guards secure the sail. You notice that, although a strong wind is howling in from the sea and snatching at your robes, the strange sail does not even flutter.

The clouds in the east appear to catch fire as the dawn breaks. Sunbeams strike the tower roof, suffusing the sail with an iridescent coral glow. Immediately it billows out as though in a mighty gale. You have guessed what is coming next, but you can still hardly believe it when it happens. The magic ship careens across the tower roof through the crumbling parapet and, with a heart-stopping lurch, sails out into space.

Turn **180**.

199

Your lightning-fast blow cuts the revolting creature nearly in two, but such is your skill that the old man is not even scratched. He blinks in bewilderment, stunned by the speed with which you acted. The spider falls to the floor. Thick fumes rise from its twitching body as it rapidly dissolves into a viscous ichor.

When there is little left but dark slime and an acrid smell, the old man says, 'There'll be another one. There always is.' He looks at you mysteriously and sighs, then he goes over to his ancient bronze treasure chest and throws open the lid. 'Here,' he says, handing you a ship in a bottle, 'this is the most powerful magic item I possess. And take this wooden flask—it contains a Potion of Wind Walking. I'll give you my Wristband of Fire, too.' He takes the copper vambrace from his wrist. Record these three items on your Character Sheet.

Not wishing to remain here with the unpredictable old man, you hurry from the room. The door slides back into place behind you as you walk on along the corridor. Turn to **288**.

200

Much to your surprise, the spell detects ho perceptible mental activity in the vicinity—apart, of course, from your own. It seems there cannot be anyone behind you after all.

Turn to **218**.

201

A worthy aim, but how do you intend to go about accomplishing it? Will you:

Swing your sword at the block of crystal?	Turn to **149**
Summon a Burning Tiger to melt it?	Turn to **104**
Use one of the items you have found?	Turn to **233**

202

The dagger appears about a metre in front of you, on the other side of the glass, and slices unerringly through the thread. You snatch up the harp as it drops and slides out into the room. Remember to note it down on your Character Sheet.

Turn to **141**.

203

Your sense of unease grows as you cross the Arena. About halfway, something makes you stop. You turn and look around you, noticing at once that the pedestal rising up from the Judicial Box is empty—the winged statue that stood atop it is gone. You drop low and start to run for the tunnel. A shadow covers the moon and you instinctively throw yourself flat as a huge winged shape hurtles overhead. You hear a hoarse saurian screech and see the ungainly bulk of a flying reptile. It is slowly climbing into the night sky for another pass, flapping its wings as though clambering up a cliff face.

You realize that your fingers are closing on the hilt of your sword. A futile reflex—you have no hope of fighting the creature while it is up in the air. It has reached the zenith of its awkward ascent and is wheeling around for the attack. Beady red eyes, filled with mindless hostility, fix their gaze on yours. Will you run (turn to **94**), or stand your ground and prepare a spell (turn to **283**)?

204

You draw your fingers across the strings, producing a scatter of plangent notes. In the ensuing silence, it seems to you that the notes still hang in the air, just beyond the range of hearing, weaving a musical spell. You watch the low spumy waves lapping in around the pebbles at your feet. The sea-foam is fired with flickering phosphorescence by the moonlight. There is no sound but the sighing of the waves and the far off whisper of the wind...

A huge glistening shape erupts out of the black water in a spray of scintillant droplets. You cry out in horror. Flinching back, you sink to your knees. You feel a terrible weakness of the spirit welling up, swamping your reason, and you maintain your composure only by the merest thread. For the first time in many years, you experience the taste of fear.

The creature before you is a grisly sight. It is like a ragged horse, but from the middle of its back grows the gnarled upper body of a huge man. Over all the body of this hybrid monster there is not a patch of skin. It is as though the misshapen body has been flayed, exposing

grotesque slabs of gory muscle, white gristle and jutting splinters of bone, veins like fat worms through which flows tarry black blood. As it rears up and smashes the pebbles in front of you with its grey hoofs, and snorts and bellows its rage to the skies, the wind blows in off the sea and brings you the smell of it. You shake with awful nausea.

'Who summons Nuckelavee?' shrieks the monster. Steam belches from its nostrils and you feel its hot foul breath on your face. 'Who dares to summon the Lord of the Waves?'

Its great hoofs could break your skull as though it were a pumpkin—and will do so, unless you act quickly. But what can you possibly do to save yourself from this fearsome demon? Will you:

Cast a spell?	Turn to **151**
Use an item?	Turn to **7**
Attack it with your sword?	Turn to **50**

205

They mutter grimly to one another. 'The coral men must not be permitted to take the Eye of the Dragon,' says one. 'We will give you what advice we can.'

'Man is the dream of a shadow,' intones another of the sphinxes. 'Lies are no less deadly than truth.'

'There are two gates through which dreams may pass,' says another. 'One of horn, the other of ivory. Those dreams that issue from the ivory gate are but fleeting illusions, but those which pass through the gate of burnished horn become reality.'

'What kind of advice is that?' you yell at them furiously. 'I need help of a more concrete nature if I'm to outwit the Kappa.'

There is a heavy sigh from the nearest sphinx. 'Very well, then, brusque mortal. Our advice to you is: return the way you came and enter the Amber Pantechnicon.'

They are prepared to say nothing more. You ponder their advice. Much of it seems to be just unhelpful nonsense, but the last suggestion is plain enough. So, will you return northwards as the sphinx said (turn to **147**), or will you continue south (turn to **210**)?

206

This time you manage to avoid the creature's snapping jaws, though you are buffeted by its wing and lose 1 point of VIGOUR. If still alive, you dive the last few metres into the safety of the tunnel.

Turn to **40**.

207

As you focus your concentration, a whirlpool of flame appears in the air between you and the advancing warriors. Within seconds the flame has coalesced into the shape of a huge tiger. In a shower of sparks it leaps upon the nearest man, and the stench of his charring flesh fills the air. The others press forward, suicidally disregarding the tiger in their effort to attack you. Its flickering claws cut a fiery swathe through them, and they fall with brief tortured cries.

As your conjuration fades and you survey the carnage, you see that one of the warriors—the sergeant—is still alive. He is sinking fast, but he seems intent on telling you something before he dies. Will you bend down to hear what it is (turn to **29**), or will you leave him and continue on into the city (turn to **48**)?

208

The door swings open and you advance into a narrow passage where carved faces gape down from the sculpted ceiling. The passage soon turns to the right. Where it bends, there is a heavy door with an ornate black lintel. A skeleton clad in mouldering garb lies across the passage.

If you use your Séance spell to contact its ghost, turn to **32**. Otherwise, will you open the door (turn to **132**), or step over the skeleton and continue along the passage (turn to **171**)?

209

As you slosh through the murky water to examine the chest, you notice a narrow tunnel in the wall. It is below the surface of the water. You could scramble along it on your hands and knees, but you would be taking a gamble on being able to hold your breath long enough to reach the other end. You decide to take a look inside the chest first, and reach out your hand towards the jewel-encrusted lid.

Turn to **24**.

210

You reach the end of the avenue. Wide broken steps descend majestically to a plaza which is almost completely submerged. Shattered columns protrude from the shimmering moonlit surface. From its height on the columns, you judge the water to be no more than waist deep. You are about to go down the steps when a party of Kappa come into view, wading across the plaza. You can hear their voices on the wind, like the notes of a reed flute. Heart pounding, you hurry away from the top of the steps.

A hollow wail pierces the night. You've been spotted. More patrols will be converging on this area, and you must get off the streets quickly. Not far to your left is the huge gaping archway that gives access to the Arena. It is not an especially inviting prospect, but at least it is preferable to staying in the open to face the spears of a hundred Kappa soldiers. With the rain in your face, you sprint towards the Arena. Turn to **12**.

211

The door at the bottom of the steps opens easily and you descend into the cellar. The low ceiling is supported by squat pillars and there are many shadowy crevices and alcoves where the light of the Orb does not reach. The floor is under a metre of oily water, the walls are furred with a moist white fungus. In a recess in the wall stands a large bronze chest studded with glittering green gems.

If you wade across to the chest, turn to **209**. If you go back to the entrance hall, turn to **107**.

212

You try to resist the hypnotic influence, but it is already eroding your will and you discover that you are unable to muster enough concentration to fight back. Your resolve suddenly crumbles and the Kappa leader's telepathic commands flood into your brain. As though in a dream, you find yourself handing over the casket. Your new master opens it and reaches for the Eye. Some part of you experiences a feeling of fury and outrage, but you no longer have any will of your own. You are the Kappa leader's slave now, and will remain so for the rest of your life. Your mission has failed.

213

Sparks fly from the spider's eyes as your sword descends, forming a mystic shield in front of the man. The force of your blow is harmlessly deflected. You turn to escape, but the loathsome spider has not finished with you yet.

Turn to **67**.

214

There are two spells which might save you. Which will you cast:

Your Gust of Wind spell? Turn to **244**
Your Invulnerability spell? Turn to **280**

If you have used both of these, you can do nothing—except brace yourself and pray. Turn to **189**.

215

The huge chunks of falling masonry crash down bare moments after you cast the protective enchantment. Miraculously you are shielded from harm. You start to laugh hysterically, tears of relief streaming down your face. Your jubilation is short lived. Your laughter turns to choked sobs as you feel the crushing weight of the heaped rubble under which you are buried. Your spell protected you for a few seconds, but when it expires you are slowly crushed as though by a giant vice. Your adventure is at an end.

216

In the darkened entrance hall, a wedge of moonlight falls upon the cringing figure of a white-haired man. He looks up and whimpers as you approach. You soon see that he is no older than yourself. From his wide staring eyes you guess that he has suffered a shock—something so terrible that it turned his hair stark white.

'Mercy,' he implores, holding forth a trembling hand. 'I am an adventurer like yourself. I came here with my friend Wulfric Stormrider. We only came in to shelter

from a storm, but when we tried to leave…' He buries his face in his hands. 'Alas! Poor Wulfric.'

It does not seem you will get more out of him for the moment, so you turn your attention to the hallway. A wide marble staircase sweeps up to the next floor, and below this a set of copper-bound double doors leads to the back of the mansion. At the other end of the hall, steps lead down to a cellar door. Will you:

Climb up to the next floor?	Turn to **99**
Go through the double doors?	Turn to **256**
Explore the cellar?	Turn to **211**

217

He takes the coins and tests each with a single yellow tooth which he has somehow kept in his rheumy jaw for just that purpose. There is a look of near disbelief in his eyes as he realizes you actually have given him two genuine gold pieces. In a whining voice he tells you he is Boolag the beggar and he has eked out a living in Thalios for several years. He does not disclose his usual source of income, nor what use he has for gold in these apparently deserted ruins.

Impatient to be on your way, you cut short his ramblings and start to brush past him. 'Watch out for Nuckelavee,' he calls after you, 'he's much worse than them coral fellers!'

This sounds interesting. You turn and look back at him. He pulls a face and stares forlornly at his two coins. If you give him another for more information, turn to **115**. If you carry on up to the Citadel, turn to **41**.

218

You whirl, risking a brief burst of light from the magic Orb to show you the face of your waylayer. To your surprise, the alleyway is empty. Then your eyes fall upon a slumped figure half hidden in a nearby doorway. You approach cautiously. When the Orb's grey light falls on the figure's face, you realize that he has been dead for several days.

'Weigh anchor, me hearties!' Another voice, different from the first, rings out. You start in alarm before noticing the emaciated mynah bird perched on the dead man's shoulder. It continues to talk as you inspect the body, and you realize that the phrases it is repeating could only have been picked up in a life of seafaring and petty villainy. The man was surely a pirate, though you cannot guess how he came to meet his end in these godforsaken ruins. His polished mahogany pegleg shines as if new in the magical light, but the rest of him is a far from pretty sight. The fingers of his left hand are closed around a green wine bottle. He seems to have nothing else of interest and you choose not to search him thoroughly.

If you take the bottle, turn to **273**. If not, turn to **243**.

219

A staircase ahead of you leads to the upper floors of the Citadel. You are about to start up it, but then you pause and reconsider. You still have to find Master Giru, and you doubt if he is anywhere in this puzzling edifice. It is time you started looking for the way out. Will you try:

A small door to your left?	Turn to **51**
A side passage to your right?	Turn to **93**

220

You find the oars hidden under some rocks in a thorn bush close to the jetty where the rowing boat is moored. You climb aboard and cast off. As you near the far side of the bay, the boat shudders and lurches to a halt. You have run aground on a sandbank. You get out and try to push the boat free, but to no avail. It has sunk too deep into the soft wet sand, and you will have to abandon it. Fortunately, it appears that the sandbank joins with the western shore of the bay. You should be able to get the rest of the way on foot.

Turn to **156**.

221

You dash to the top of the winding flight of stairs and begin the dizzying descent to the floor of the hall. Lord Mantiss screams in rage. It is a horrible, subhuman sound. Despite yourself, you pause and look back over your shoulder. Your bizarre adversary has not finished with you yet—he is perched on the edge of the balustrade, and as you watch he leaps out from the balcony towards you. His maroon robes spread out as he sails incredibly through the air, doubtless propelled by legs more grasshopper than human. You have time for one spell before he lands on the step in front of you. Will it be:

The Gust of Wind spell?	Turn to **197**
The Deadly Swarm spell?	Turn to **232**
The Burning Tiger spell?	Turn to **266**

If you have cast all of these, you have no recourse but to stand and fight it out—turn to **231**.

222

The foul creature drops into the darkness below. Missing the rusted spikes, it hits the oily water and sinks without trace. It has suffered the very fate it intended for you. You return to the entrance hall.

Turn to **152**.

223

You rush over to the wall and scramble through the breach. Behind you, the bronze statue comes to a halt; it is too big to get through the narrow gap. Relieved at your lucky escape, you peer around you at the empty moonlit streets. No Kappa in sight—you can continue south.

A low, deep creaking sound makes you turn. The bronze statue is pushing against the wall with its metallic sinews. Its blank eyes return your gaze with an implacable stare. Unbelievably, the wall is starting to topple! Cracks appear and spread across the grey-white stone. With a groan of ancient rock, the wall collapses. Blocks of masonry cascade at your feet as you jump back, and the bronze warrior advances through the debris.

Terror transfixes you. Your only hope is the Burning Tiger spell. If you have not used this yet, now is the time to cast it (turn to **140**). If you used the spell earlier, turn to **117**.

224

As your spell expires, the tiger's flames fade and it dissipates into thin air. Although seared and torn by the battle, the warrior-god idol still stands. It sways as it scans the hall for you. Smoke rises from the joints in its armour. For a moment you think it might fall, crippled by the damage it has taken, but then it points its swords towards you and lurches forward.

IDOL   VIGOUR 3

Roll two dice:

score 2 to 3   You are hit four times; lose 12 VIGOUR
score 4 to 5   You are hit three times; lose 9 VIGOUR
score 6   You take two hits; lose 6 VIGOUR
score 7   You are hit once and lose 3 VIGOUR
score 8 to 12   The idol loses 3 VIGOUR

If you defeat it, turn to **303**.

225

The entrance hall is built on a massive scale, and even the light of the Orb does not reach beyond the towering pillars to the ceiling high above. The walls are decorated with a swirling tracery of inlaid silver.

Seeing a corridor not far away, you head along it. After a short distance you come to a bossed metal door in the wall to your left. If you stop at the door, turn to **96**. If you walk on, turn to **288**.

226

You feel suddenly weightless. The gloating faces of the gloomviles recede and vanish as you seem to plummet along a swirling tunnel of misty lights. You feel dizzy and disorientated, and your mystic senses tell you that some sorcery of a forgotten nature is at work. The spinning lights are making you feel sick, and you screw your eyes tight shut.

After a minute or two you open them again. You are now lying on the plaza just inside the main gate of Thalios. Your VIGOUR, AGILITY and PSI are back to their normal scores. The only items you now possess are your sword, your flask of drinking water, the Orb of Illumination and your bag containing 10 gold pieces, You have been flung back through time to the point at which your adventure began! All your spells have now returned—and perhaps you will use them more wisely now, with your knowledge of what lies ahead.

Like ghosts from the past, the four warriors who formed your 'honour guard' are approaching with swords drawn. You scramble to your feet, cursing the inevitability of this sorry combat. Turn to **53**.

227

The warriors stare blankly back at you as though they do not understand. As you move to pass them, they crouch down in fighting posture and close in on you. Your hand is on your sword-hilt, and the black blade leaps from its scabbard with a metallic whisper. Will you fight them (turn to **53**), or first try one of your spells (turn to **282**)?

228

The door opens and, with an elegant gesture, the hand motions you to step inside. You enter a room lit by a single lantern. Two guards wearing the livery of the Academy flank the door. They turn to face you, hands flying to their swords, but the third man in the room

waves them away. He is in his sixties and wears the austere robes of the Academy. He has a heavy build that suggests he may have been a fighter in his youth, but he has the kindly eyes of a scholar. It can be none other than Master Giru.

The hand smugly points you out to Giru, then flits over to him and shrinks until it is small enough to enter a ring on his finger. He snaps the clasp of the ring shut to seal it in. 'Welcome,' says Giru, taking you by the hand. 'We feared the Kappa had got you,' He sees you staring at his ring. 'Ah, you are bewildered by the scout I sent looking for you. That was Sinistrum. He's a genie—or rather, the last bit of one. The rest of him was destroyed in a magical duel six centuries ago, but I found the hand in a jar I dug up on one of my archaeological expeditions. He is a good servant for simple tasks, though he will spitefully misinterpret any complex or important command. Still, come and sit down. You look as though you've been through hell to get here.'

You gratefully take a swig from the brandy flask he pushes into your hand. 'Did you meet up with the four men I sent to bring you here?' he continues.

The look in your eyes gives him his answer, and he hangs his head sadly. The guards' faces are dark and grim.

'Tomorrow there will be time for mourning,' you tell them. 'Our immediate priority is to escape from the ruins with the Eye.'

Giru surprises you by telling you that he does not have the Eye here. 'It is still in its casket atop the Vault of Heroes, on a promontory to the west. I considered it dangerous to move even the unopened casket before you got here.'

You jump to your feet. 'Then what are we sitting around here for? We must get to the Eye quickly, before the Kappa find it.'

Giru shakes his head and waves you back to your

chair. 'Too late for that, I'm afraid. They found it hours ago, when they first came out of the ocean and surprised us. Still, that isn't as bad as it sounds. The last thing I did was to activate a force field device that I'd already set up around the Eye as a safety measure. That force field will prevent the Kappa from reaching the Eye, and the device is not set to turn itself off until several hours after sunrise. We may as well get some sleep now. The Kappa are accustomed to a dim, watery light, so dawn will give us at least one advantage over them.'

You are forced to admit that Giru's suggestions make sense. The four of you settle down as comfortably as you can in the spartan room. You find, however, that sleep does not come easily. Your mind is awhirl with thoughts of the coming day. You may be facing the greatest battle of your life—and, as yet, you have no inkling of how you are going to win it. You yawn, feeling all the fatigue of the last few hours.

Turn to **277**.

229

One of the Kappa utters an anxious inhuman cry as you charge, but the other coolly levels his magical sceptre and shoots a second blast of energy.

In order to dodge this you must roll equal to or less than your current AGILITY on two dice. If you succeed, turn to **184**. If the dice score exceeds your AGILITY, turn to **278**.

230

You scramble through the archway. The shadows pour through behind you like a pack of slavering hounds. Depth and colour appear in each shadow as it issues through the archway. They are becoming real. Instead of mere shadows, twenty fierce gladiators now surround you. Witch-lights dance on the prongs of their long tridents. One throws a heavy net to entangle you. There are too many of them. Knowing you are about to die, you draw your sword. You sell your life dearly in a blazing display of sorcery and swordplay, a true scion of the Elder Realm.

231

Lord Mantiss alights in front of you like a huge locust. There is no escape now—you have no option but to pit your heavy black blade against the blurring speed of his rapier.

Roll two dice:

score 2	He pierces your heart, killing you instantly
score 3 to 7	You are hit and lose 3 VIGOUR
score 8 to 12	Lord Mantiss loses 3 VIGOUR

If you win, turn to **122**.

232

The hornets hover in an angrily seething cloud, waiting for Mantiss to alight on the steps in front of you. 'Blackhearted zcroundrel,' chortles the insect-man, 'you are undone by the very zpell you would have zent againzt me. Know you not?—I am the Lord of Inzectz!'

Terror seizes your heart with an icy grip as you see the buzzing hornets descend towards you at Mantiss's command. Before you can run or attempt another spell, the hornets are upon you. Thousands of fatal stings sink into your flesh. As you fall to your knees, Lord Mantiss kicks your pain-wracked body off the staircase and you plunge to your death in the hall below.

233

You can think of at most two items which might prove useful. If you have them, you can try either a jewelled harp (turn to **195**) or a bottle of vinegar (turn to **167**). Failing that, you could cast your Burning Tiger spell (turn to **104**) if you have not yet used it, or you could simply hack at the block with your sword (turn to **149**).

When the lid of the snuff box is opened, a loud screech comes from inside. You almost drop the box in shock. Since the deafening shriek shows no signs of abating, you snap the lid shut. The noise stops immediately.

You can now eat the pomegranate (turn to **13**) or the golden apple (turn to **253**), or leave the cellar (turn to **82**).

They leaf through their rulebook, explaining that they have not played this game for some centuries. It seems that in Mix-Up you must stake points of either AGILITY or PSI. Suppose you were to stake 2 points of PSI. If you won, these points would be transferred from your PSI score to your AGILITY score. If you lost, however, you would forfeit the 2 points of PSI. It is possible to increase a characteristic above its normal score playing Mix-Up, but you are not allowed to make a wager that might put your AGILITY or PSI above 10 or below 3.

After deciding whether to stake AGILITY or PSI, and how many points you will stake, you must guess a number between 2 and 12. Now roll two dice. If the total is the number you guessed, you transfer the points you staked from AGILITY to PSI (or vice versa). If your guess was only 1 out (eg, if you guessed a 7 and rolled an 8), nothing is gained or lost. If you guessed any other number, you lose the points you staked.

Play one game of Mix-Up (you may play more if you wish). After this, you can either try a different game (return to **42** and choose again) or continue on your way (turn to **208**).

It is a Glove of Unerring Dexterity. As long as you wear it, you add 1 to every Combat Roll you make during a fight. (If, for example, you were to roll a 7 in combat then you would count this as an 8.) Furthermore, if you score a double 6 in any Combat Round then this means you have struck right through your opponent's guard, killing him/her/it instantly.

You are extremely lucky to have come across a magic item of such power. With a spring in your step, you make your way back to the ground floor. Turn to **241**.

237

You summon up all your reserves of willpower and manage to shrug off the hypnotic thrall into which you were being drawn. The Kappa leader seems amazed at your ability to resist his psionic power. You take advantage of his surprise to pull free of his grip.

Turn to **154**.

238

No sooner have you stepped into the room than a steel trap springs up from the floor and closes agonizingly on your leg. You may use your Invulnerability spell if you still have it, but otherwise you lose 1 AGILITY and 2 VIGOUR points.

If you are still alive, you take hold of the trap and force it open long enough to get your wounded leg free. There is nothing else of interest in this small room—a fact which merely adds indignation to injury. You back out and try the other door.

Turn to **84**.

239

The remaining Kappa fights on. You seem to sense a reddish glow of bloodlust in the pale nacreous sheen of its eyes.

Roll two dice:

score 2 to 5	You are wounded—lose 3 VIGOUR
score 6 to 12	The Kappa loses 3 VIGOUR

You now have a chance to *flee* south towards the Avenue of Sphinxes—turn to **304** if so. If you continue the fight and win, turn to **133**.

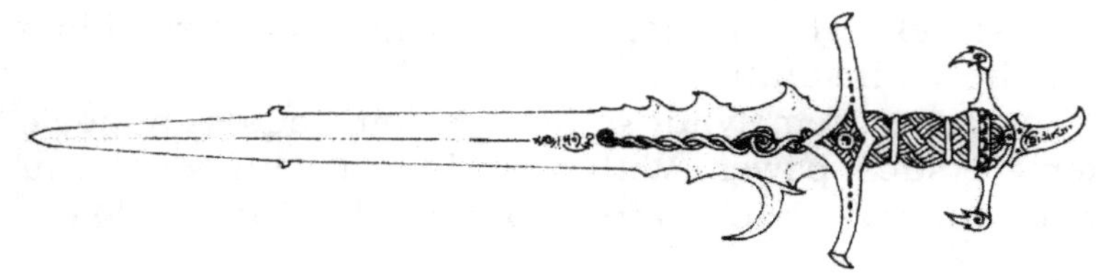

You glance again at your map. You have only to go along a narrow cobbled passage between two buildings and you should be at the Palatine Bridge. The passage is roofed over, but the cold wind that howls through it means that there is little shelter here from the insistent drizzle. The passage is draped in a sepulchral gloom, and echoes eerily to the sound of your boots on the damp cobblestones. You are drawing close to the end when a tall figure drifts into view in front of you. She wears extravagant robes of grey and blue; billowed up by the wind, the folds of her dark mantle almost brush your face. Her expression and bearing are serene, yet somehow terrible. You sense no human soul in her, and your hand goes automatically to your sword.

'Well, little mortal,' she says, her voice like a javelin of ice. 'Where are you going in such a hurry? To stop the coral men from finding what they seek? You alone, against their legions?' Her pitiless laughter rings out along the passage.

You draw the sword. Moonlight sends a shiver of ebon light along its blade. 'Madam, my mission is important and I must not be delayed. Please stand aside.' You try to sound stern and implacable, but the effect is spoiled somewhat by a nervous quaver in your voice.

'Your mission is futile. Embrace despair. Learn to love her.'

As you raise your sword defiantly, she begins a strange lilting chant. You know who she is now—Ligea, demi-goddess of despair. Her mournful song drives all hope from your heart. With each sad note that escapes

from her lips, you become more convinced that your quest is futile. Your sword clatters on the ground and you slump beside it. You must do something, while you still have the will to act. Will you:

Open a mother-of-pearl snuffbox?	Turn to **254**
Cast a Mind Shield spell?	Turn to **279**
Eat a pomegranate?	Turn to **13**

If you have none of these, you give in completely to Ligea's insidious song and lie here until you rot.

241

You wait until the Kappa have all gone and then edge cautiously around the quadrangle. The moon hangs mistily above the drizzle; its reflection is a silvery smear on the wet ground. Twice you have to retreat back into the darkness of broken doorways to avoid Kappa patrols, but eventually you reach the point where you first entered the quadrangle.

Without warning, a black shape almost a metre across darts out of the shadows nearby and swiftly moves towards you. It makes a sound like bones rattling together as it runs.

Before you can react, or even discern the details of its form, it has reached you. A stabbing pain lances up your leg. Lose 2 VIGOUR and, if you are still alive, turn to **60**.

242

You step through open doors into the building. You are in a large hall. The sprawling Palace corridors stretch off into the distance to either side.

Will you turn right, and make your way towards the west tower (turn to **168**), or left, and make your way towards the south tower (turn to **101**)?

243

You can take his pegleg if you wish. Who knows, it may come in handy. Remember to note it down on your

Character Sheet if you do.

As you turn to go on your way, the scrawny mynah bird flutters up to alight on your shoulder. Will you brush it away and leave alone (turn to **144**), or continue with it as a companion (turn to **257**)?

244

Wind from out of nowhere roars up the chute as you descend. You slide gradually down the last few metres and emerge gently into the room at the bottom.

Turn to **38**.

245

The prosopteryx flies straight into the buzzing black cloud of hornets created by your spell—and emerges utterly unscathed. The stings of mere insects, even those formed by sorcery, are insufficient to pierce the stony skin of this hell-spawned creature. You must rely on your sword.

Turn to **43**.

246

The figurine has a small catch on the back of its head which you are able to turn. No sooner have you done this than it twists out of your hands and grows rapidly to become a squat metallic fighter about a metre tall. With a ringing war cry it rushes towards you, cold hatred shining in its tiny pearl eyes. It compensates for its small stature with a powerful combat style that incorporates leaping kicks and powerful blows from its club-like fists.

SILVER FIGURINE   VIGOUR 12

Roll two dice:
score 2 to 5   You are hit; lose 3 VIGOUR
score 6 to 12   The silver figurine loses 3 VIGOUR

If you *flee* along the corridor, turn to **288**. If you destroy your opponent, turn to **262**.

247

You come to a small room which is empty apart from two alabaster jars on a shelf. You unstopper them and examine the contents. One of them is a mystery to you, but you identify the other as a Potion of Wind Walking. Since there is no other exit from this room, you take the jars and return the way you came.

Reaching the skeleton, it suddenly occurs to you that you could use the Potion of Wind Walking to get safely across the pool of darkness. If you do, turn to **155**. If you go back downstairs, turn to **88**.

248

You select what you believe to be the proper frequency and begin to focus your mind upon it.

Turn to **86**.

249

The leathery creature only catches you a glancing blow, but its long teeth still inflict a nasty wound across your back. Lose 2 VIGOUR points and, if you are still alive, turn to **66**.

250

Lord Mantiss watches you askance with his sparkling faceted eyes as you leave the treasure room. You have the weird impression that he is disgruntled by your choice of item. He drops the huge block back into place. It crunches down heavily, just missing your toes. 'Now go,' sighs Mantiss with a heavy heart. You back away at his waspish gesture and hurry down through a series of ramshackle halls to the ground floor.

Turn to **241**.

251

The pegleg lodges in the hemophage's mouth. It tries to force its jaws shut, but this only makes the hard wood prod more deeply into the soft flesh of its mouth.

Blinded by tears of pain, it stumbles off along the corridor, desperately pulling at the pegleg with its clumsy taloned fingers.

Turn to **76**.

252

[Illustration on next page]

As you proceed, you begin to suspect that something is following you. What starts as a vague unease begins to gel into certainty as you hear soft padding footfalls echoing along the corridor. Each time you stop to listen, your pursuer stops as well. You quietly slide your sword from its scabbard and walk on, straining to hear the creature's footsteps. It is getting closer, doubtless hoping to creep up on you unawares. Your fingers tighten on the sword-hilt. You are ready for it.

There is a harsh, guttural roar and a rush of heavy footsteps. You start to whirl, thinking that with any luck it might impale itself on your waiting blade. The triumphant smile leaves your face as the sword is suddenly jerked up out of your hands and pinned to the roof of the tunnel by an invisible force.

Disarmed, you find yourself face to face with a hemophage—a crouched, half-human monstrosity with long jagged claws and a grinning crocodile head. Its body is drenched in the gore of its victims—and you will be the next, unless you think quickly.

Will you fight it with your bare hands (turn to **92**), cast a spell (turn to **14**), or reach into your backpack for an item (turn to **285**)?

253

As soon as you bite into the fruit you recognize it as a Proteus Pome, whose magical juice carries a spell of transformation. You cry out as the spell takes hold of you and your body is swiftly warped and altered into the shape of a majestic golden eagle. You soar about the cellar several times, flying back to the chest only when

you feel the magic wearing off and your normal form returning. The flesh of the fruit no longer has its former golden hue—one bite is enough to drain it of magic, and it is now just a common apple. You eat it and discard the core before turning your attention to the other items that were in the chest.

If you have not yet done so, you can now eat the pomegranate (turn to **13**) or open the snuff box (turn to **234**). Alternatively you can ascend the cellar steps to the entrance hall (turn to **82**).

254

A deafening screech is emitted from the box the moment you lift the lid. The noise is so loud that it completely drowns out Ligea's disheartening chant. You retrieve your sword and march past her. She says something to you as she fades back to her own dismal world, but you cannot hear her over the box's noise. When you are sure she has gone, you snap it shut.

Turn to **284**.

255

Hoping to move them to compassion, you blurt out a tale of looking for your long-lost brother, whom you claim was abducted by the Kappa. The sphinxes seem unmoved. 'Complete your quest and leave these sad ruins,' says one stonily. 'Thalios is not a stage for the petty dramas of mortals.'

Their flinty stares make you feel uncomfortable, and you hurry on your way. Turn to **210**.

256

You almost trip over something in the gloom—a large, badly chipped battleaxe. It is not this which draws your attention, however, but the corpse lying on the floor in front of you. A few days ago he must have been a burly armour-clad mountain of a man. Now he is nothing but dead meat. The white-haired adventurer groans as you activate the Orb of Illumination and reluctantly stoop to inspect the body. The sight makes your gorge rise. It has no head.

Turn to **135**.

257

You step out of the alley into a large quadrangle dominated by the ruins of a huge domed building—the Amber Pantechnicon. Around the perimeter of the quadrangle, the cobblestones are littered with broken tiles which have fallen from the crumbling roofs.

About fifty metres away, their thin coral bodies gleaming darkly in the moonlight, two Kappa are patrolling the quadrangle. You slip back into the concealing shadows as they begin to move in your direction. They seem not to notice you and walk straight past where you are hiding, but then the wretched mynah squawks, 'Look lively, you bilge rats!' The Kappa look round, peering into the shadows with their huge pearl eyes. Their hands are reaching for their weapons.

Turn to **5**.

258

You start to make your way along a narrow alley. The buildings to either side lean crazily together so that only a narrow chink of coal-black sky is visible above. The darkness here is absolute. It occurs to you to use light from your Orb of Illumination—but that could attract decidedly unwanted attention if there are more of the appalling Kappa about. You resort to feeling your way slowly along the rough stone wall. The alley twists and turns and is joined by innumerable side streets, but you head doggedly west.

There is the metallic scrape of a sword being drawn—right behind your back. You freeze and an icy tingle runs down your spine. A gruff voice says, 'Now then, matey, just drop your moneybag and you won't get hurt.'

Will you:

Do as you are told?   Turn to **165**
Cast a spell?   Turn to **21**
Draw your sword and
   turn to face the man?   Turn to **218**

259

You ascend to the alcove. The bowl is fashioned from a giant, gleaming clam shell. A wad of silken fabric lies within. You soon discover that this is actually a large sheet of silvery-white material. It is light and strong, but so thin that it can be folded into a space not much bigger than your fist. You slip the fabric into your backpack and hurry back along the hall before your protective spell wears off.

Will you explore the mansion further (turn to **171**), or go back downstairs (turn to **88**)?

260

There is a loud clang as your enchanted sword strikes home. You might as well have used a twig for all the effect your blow has on the statue's impervious body. Its fist flies out and deals you a stunning blow. You are thrown back sprawling in the long grass.

Lose 4 VIGOUR points. If you are still alive, you jump up quickly as the giant warrior lumbers closer. Turn to **223**.

261

Chu lifts the conical shell—to reveal a fat, gleaming pearl. He starts in astonishment, not realizing it is merely an illusion. The large round spider fidgets and watches you mistrustfully, turning this way and that to bring you under the scrutiny of each of its wine-dark eyes.

'Extraordinary!' gasps Chu at last. 'I can't imagine how you knew. Still, I'm a man of my word...' He reaches into a corroded bronze chest behind him and brings out a ship in a bottle, which he hands to you. 'Since you are a friend of Mantiss, and a true adept in the art of obfuscation, I don't at all mind letting you have this.'

You thank him and leave the room to head further into the Citadel. Turn to **288**.

262

The figurine gives a tinny groan and shrinks back to its normal size. You will have something to say to Mantiss about his gift, should you happen to run into that peculiar insect-man again.

Finally deciding that there is nothing you can do to open the strange door, you continue onwards. Turn to **288**.

263

Only your years of training in the ways of wizardry might save you now. The Kappa leader's hypnosis is a particularly potent form of psychic attack, and you must resist it as you would a hostile spell.

Roll two dice. If the total is greater than your current PSI score, turn to **212**. If the dice roll is equal to or less than your PSI, turn to **237**.

264

The moonbeams seem to cluster and coagulate into the shimmering form of one of the warriors. It is the sergeant's ghost. It drifts slowly towards you. Suffering shows in its sad eyes, its drawn face. It tears at its clothes and hair, and speaks to you imploringly: 'Send me back. I cannot bear to live again.'

'Answer one question and I shall release you. Where in the Palace is Master Giru's camp?'

'Giru...' answers the ghost as though struggling to recapture a dim memory. 'He was my master. We hid from the Kappa in a room in the west tower. The door had a colour, but I can no longer remember colours.'

'Give me more precise directions,' you demand, but the ghost is already fading from view. Obviously it was unacquainted with the etiquette of Séance. With nothing else to go on, you enter the Palace's west tower. Turn to **168**.

265

You swing the hard obsidian pommel of your sword against the pane with all your strength. You feel the jarring impact through your whole body, but the glass is enchanted and does not shatter. The harp dangles tantalizingly on the other side of the pane. You bite your lip as you consider resorting to magic but, in the event, you are not given the chance—

Turn to **141**.

266

Lord Mantiss alights on the steps on front of you just as the tiger materializes in answer to your summons. 'Fey villain!' declares Mantiss. 'Your trickery will not zave you now.'

As he bounds up the stairs towards you, the tiger prowls forward to block his path. Mantiss darts and weaves, and although the tiger manages to strike him once or twice you soon see that it is the insect-man who has the upper hand. Their battle blocks the staircase. Your only means of escape would be to jump down to the floor, and it is a long way down from here.

If you risk the jump, turn to **177**. If you stand where you are and wait for the fight to end, turn to **291**.

267

The gloomvile demands an item from your backpack. If you want to play another game, you must hand over an item and return to **42** to make your choice. You must not part with your sword or the Orb of Illumination— these items are vital to your quest.

If you aren't willing to part with an item, you had better hurry from the room through the far door (turn to **208**).

268

You decide that it is not worth using your magic against a lone opponent, so you leap out in front of the Kappa wielding your black sword. To defend itself, it draws a

wide-bladed shortsword from the dolphin-skin harness
it is wearing.

KAPPA   VIGOUR 12

Roll two dice:
score 2 to 5   You are wounded; lose 3 VIGOUR
score 6 to 12   The Kappa loses 3 VIGOUR

If you win, turn to **274**.

269

A sheet of incandescent flame erupts from the copper
wristband towards the ceiling. You concentrate to bring
the flame under control and focus it into a narrow
searing arc. The plate begins to shine red-hot and the
sword drops with a clang at your feet.

You have used up all the energy stored in the
Wristband of Fire, and must cross it off your Character
Sheet. Your sword is also quite hot by now. You wait
until it has cooled down enough to touch, and continue
on your way. Turn to **308**.

270

This idol is animated by the power of an ancient god of
warriors. Can you really hope to beat it in a straight
fight?

IDOL   VIGOUR 15

Roll two dice:
score 2 to 3   You are hit four times; lose 12 VIGOUR
score 4 to 5   You are hit three times; lose 9 VIGOUR
score 6   You are hit twice; lose 6 VIGOUR
score 7   You are hit once and lose 3 VIGOUR
score 8 to 12   The idol loses 3 VIGOUR

You can turn to *flee* out through the courtyard to the
plaza (turn to **274**), but if you do so and fail the AGILITY
roll then the idol will hit you with all four of its swords,
inflicting a 12 point wound to your VIGOUR.

If you fight on and somehow win, turn to **303**.

271

Within the chest you find a golden apple, a pomegranate and a small mother-of-pearl snuff box. Take any of these that you wish. If you intend to examine them here and now, will you:

Open the snuffbox?	Turn to **234**
Eat the golden apple?	Turn to **253**
Eat the pomegranate ?	Turn to **13**

If you return to the entrance hall, turn to **82**.

272

There is no time to think of anything terribly clever—you just create the illusion of a brick wall directly in the path of the swooping monster. It flaps its heavy wings ponderously in an attempt to swerve, and careens into the ground. It hisses furiously and begins to struggle into take-off position. On the Arena floor it is you who have the advantage; you draw your sword and rush to do battle with the grounded beast.

Turn to **49**.

273

You uncork it and sniff at the contents. The smell is not of wine, but vinegar. A curious thing for a man to carry around with him.

Will you risk a drink from the bottle? If so, turn to **294**. If not, turn to **243**.

274

The moon is rising above the shattered city walls, sketching out the ruins of Thalios with wan bars of light. A cold wind blows across the open plaza. Your eyes fall upon the constellation known to your people as the Thurifer, or the Pious Acolyte. It is high in the sky—a good omen. You feel exposed out on the vast empty plaza, and you are anxious to reach somewhere more secluded before another Kappa comes along.

Do you head directly south across the Bridge of Blue Skulls (turn to **108**), or do you make for the warren of narrow streets to the west (turn to **258**)?

275

You frantically mouth the phrases of the spell, and the air around you responds by forming a shrieking blast of wind to push against the falling pillar. Sadly, not even this conjured hurricane is enough to hold up tonnes of rock. You can only watch helplessly as the huge chunks of marble crash down, pulverizing the life from you. Your adventure ends here.

276

The robed figure stands motionless for a few moments before clambering gingerly out of the ruins of his icy prison. His gangling body seems oddly misshapen under the folds of heavy maroon cloth, and for some reason he is wearing a large black mask with overlapping face-plates and eye-slits set with faceted lenses. It is only when he speaks, and you see the plates at the bottom of the mask whirring in motion, that you understand that it is not a mask at all. It is the face of a gigantic insect.

'Ezzteemed friend!' says the insect-man in a buzzing imitation of human speech. 'You have freed me from a mozt unpleazzant incarzeration. For thiz, you have the gratitude of Lord Mantizz. Let me take you down to my treazure room, where we can dizcuzz your reward.'

He heads off towards the stairs, beckoning you to

follow with a sweep of his knobbly chitinous hand. On the other hand, you notice, he wears a glowing silver gauntlet.

Lord Mantiss leads you down one flight of stairs and then through a maze of drear galleries. At last the two of you emerge on to a balcony high above a marble-floored hall. Lord Mantiss pauses for a moment as if sunk in thought, then his long arms reach out to encircle a huge chunk of masonry which he lifts up as though it were made of straw. A narrow doorway is revealed in the wall behind the block.

'My zecret treazure room,' announces Lord Mantiss, inclining his head towards the dark doorway. 'Pray enter and zelect what pleazzes you.'

Will you go through the doorway (turn to **71**), or will you refuse to do as he asks (turn to **105**)?

277

'It is time to leave,' says Master Giru, waking you. Several hours have passed and a wan, grey predawn light now filters into the room. 'We have a problem,' he continues. The promontory on which the Vault of Heroes stands is completely cordoned off by a force of at least fifty Kappa. I have just been up to the roof of the tower and seen them for myself. The only way we could reach the Eye would be to fly across.'

You explain that none of your spells gives the power of flight, but you may have an item that will help. You lay out all the items you have collected in the course of your adventure and go over them one by one with the knowledgeable old scholar.

Do you have a ship in a bottle *and* a sheet of strange fabric? If so turn to **198**. If you do not have both of these items, turn to **35**.

278

The sceptre's discharge crackles through the musty air, momentarily illuminating the ancient chamber with a harsh and ghastly light. You try to twist away from the bolt, but too slowly. It rips through your leg and you scream in pain.

Lose 8 VIGOUR points and 1 AGILITY point. If you are still alive, you manage to stagger on and swing your sword at the Kappa. Turn to **39**.

279

You can still hear Ligea's eldritch song, but you are protected from it now by the spell. You retrieve your sword and stride past her. She sweeps regally away and begins to fade, returning to her own dismal realm. Her last words stay to vex you: 'Foolish mortal! I brought you truth…'

Turn to **284**.

280

You fly out of the bottom of the chute at terrifying speed. You cannot help wincing as you go hurtling across the room and collide with the far wall. Fortunately, the spell shields you from injury. You land dusty but unhurt.

Turn to **38**.

281

Whose ghost will you summon? You might try the beggar you met on the Bridge of Blue Skulls, in which case turn to **100**. If he has not died since you encountered him then the spell will be wasted, of course.

If you have come across the body of a one-legged pirate during your adventure, then you could attempt to call upon his ghost—in which case, turn to **46**.

282

You can cast either Burning Tiger (turn to **207**) or The Deadly Swarm (turn to **75**).

283

Will you cast:

Your Befuddle spell?	Turn to **173**
Your Gust of Wind spell?	Turn to **190**
Your Mirage spell?	Turn to **272**

If you have used all of these already, you had better run for it (turn to **94**).

284

The Palantine Bridge, which once spanned one of the magnificent canals of ancient Thalios, is now a ruined structure of weathered marble. It is the only link between the city and the Consul's Palace, from where Thalios was ruled in ages past. You gaze out towards the Palace. Giru is there; you can feel it. Picking your way carefully around the yawning cracks in the stonework, you begin to cross the bridge.

There is a blur of motion ahead. Something flashes in the moonlight. Your instinct takes over and you hurl yourself to one side. Your lightning reactions save you from certain death, but the hurtling spear still catches you a glancing blow across the shoulder. Lose 3 VIGOUR points.

If you are still alive, you prepare to battle two Kappa that are rushing towards you. Hard on their coral heels come three sentinel crabs, scuttling along eagerly to assist their inhuman masters at the kill. You are badly outnumbered.

Will you cast a spell to even the odds (turn to **33**), or trust to your warrior skills (turn to **309**)?

285

There are three items which might prove useful now, if you have them. Will you try:

A Wristband of Fire?   Turn to **113**
A pirate's pegleg?   Turn to **138**
The spine of a prosopteryx?   Turn to **172**

If you have none of these, or choose not to use them, will you cast a spell (turn to **14**), or will you resort to fighting with your bare hands (turn to **92**)?

286

He lifts the conical shell with a triumphant flourish. There is no pearl there. Before you have a chance to examine the other shells, he has swept the whole lot from the table into his lap.

You feel cheated. If you threaten him with your sword, turn to **188**. If you can accept your loss gracefully, hand over the item you wagered and then continue on your way by turning to **288**.

287

Fear and darkness rush in on you. You scream as a whirlpool of spectral faces leer from the shadows like moths around a guttering candle. Arcane necromancy drives you to the brink of insanity.

Roll two dice, and pray that the score does not exceed your current PSI. If it does, turn to **187**. If the dice roll is equal to or less than your current PSI, turn to **301**.

288

The corridor turns to the right and you follow it on into a wide gallery that stretches ahead of you. The wall panels and pinewood beams have taken on a rich lustre with age. A flood of cheerless amber light comes from a giant crystal with twenty glowing facets which hangs in the air in the middle of the gallery. You approach with caution. It is producing a low humming, and every so often spins around into a new orientation". It is

obviously far too big to take with you, even if you knew a way to cancel out the force which keeps it hovering above the floor, so you start towards the far end of the gallery.

It seems to you that the humming from the crystal abruptly changes in pitch. Something moves at the edge of your vision—tall shadows, leaping wildly along the panelled walls as the crystal turns. They look like gaunt yammering demons glimpsed in a dream. One of the shadows advances noiselessly across the wooden floor like a slithering snake. Without really thinking about it, you find yourself running for the end of the gallery. The capering shadows keep pace with you, flitting in a mad tangle across walls, floor and ceiling, converging on the two archways you can see ahead of you. Their rushing shapes form a weird pattern, like swaying seaweed. Or a closing web.

You are nearly at the end of the room. You are running like the wind, but your mind is clear and free of panic. You consider the two archways ahead of you. Both seem to lead into the same chamber beyond, but one is framed by giant antlers while the sweeping tusks of a mammoth enclose the other. Will you pass through the archway with the frame of antlers (turn to **230**), or the archway with the frame of tusks (turn to **176**)?

289

You pull the bottle from your backpack and swing it with all your strength at the Kappa leader's head. It shatters against his helmet, splashing vinegar into his eyes. The vinegar eats into the pearl eyes like acid. The Kappa falls back with a horrible wail. With his concentration broken you are free of the hypnotic assault.

Turn to **154**.

290

The creature's jaws close around your flesh, ripping a bloody chunk from your arm. Agonizing pain lances through your whole body. Lose 5 VIGOUR points.

If you are still alive, you manage to stay conscious and stumble the last few paces into the tunnel leading from the Arena. Turn to **40**.

291

You are flabbergasted to see Mantiss defeat your tiger of flame. No one has ever done that before. But his robes are charred and smeared with soot. Scorched by the tiger's fire, he climbs unsteadily towards you. Now is your chance to finish him off.

LORD MANTISS   VIGOUR 3

Roll two dice:
score 2   A critical thrust slays you at once
score 3 to 7 You are wounded; lose 3 VIGOUR
score 8 to 12 Mantiss loses 3 VIGOUR

If you win, turn to **122**.

292

As you planned, the sudden blast of wind catches the flying creature unawares and dashes it against the obsidian wall. You give it no chance to recover. Reversing your grip on your sword, you plunge it down deep into the creature's forehead. A fleeting scream of thwarted bloodlust rings out, and then the monstrous thing is still. Under your incredulous gaze it crumbles like a weathered alabaster bust.

Turn to **119**.

293

Will you cast:

Dagger of the Mind?   Turn to **202**
Gust of Wind?   Turn to **307**

If you have neither of these, or do not want to use them, turn to **141**.

294

You take only a few drops of the vinegar, but regrettably that is more than enough. You reel and fall to the hard cobblestones as if hit with a belaying pin. Unknown to you, a treacherous colleague of the dead pirate poisoned his wine. The poison which slowly turned the wine to vinegar killed him when he drank it—just as it is now killing you. All your fighting prowess and your skill at sorcery cannot save you. The black cloak of Death envelops you…

'Shiver me timbers!' exclaims the mynah.

295

You place ten gold pieces on the altar stone in front of the idol. Nothing happens. You consider taking back the money, but decide against it. A wise person is careful never to anger the gods, for who knows when one might need the luck they can bestow?

If you go back to the plaza, turn to **274**. If you first try lighting the braziers, turn to **106**.

296

The mynah bird immediately drops the Orb beside it on the parapet and begins to stare about quizzically. As you step forward, it fixes you with a cross-eyed glare and then launches itself out into space. You watch it flap crazily away across the quadrangle as though drunk.

Turn to **306**.

297

You reach out and extinguish the nearest candle. One of the gloomviles immediately throws up his hands and shrieks, then vanishes in a puff of grey smoke. A whiff of brimstone hangs in the air. The other two gloomviles wring their hands and plead with you, but you know them to be irredeemable beings who deserve no mercy. You snuff out another candle, and a second gloomvile disappears. Ignoring the snarled threats of the third, you skirt around the confining pentacle to the last candle and cheerfully blow it out. The echo of a howl hangs in the air, and then there is silence.

Just as you are about to go on your way, you notice a small ivory plaque lying in the middle of the pentacle. If you pick this up, turn to **56**. If you ignore it and head for the door in the opposite wall, turn to **208**.

298

You intone the spell and a seething cloud of droning hornets hangs in the dank air. The Kraken quickly retreats under the surface, away from the pain of their lashing stings. You know that the spell will not last long, so you hurry up the cellar steps before the lurking Kraken can re-emerge from the water.

Turn to **107**.

299

As you cross the lawn, you have a sudden feeling that something is amiss. Thoughts racing, you look around you. The pedestal by the door is empty—the statue has moved! A shouted warning from the mansion comes just in time; you throw yourself flat on the grass as a huge bronze fist cleaves the air just above your head. You look up to see the statue towering over you, grim and black against the cloudy sky. It raises a heavy armoured foot to crush you. You will die if you do not roll aside in time—but you find you cannot move. Fear has drained your strength.

A bellowing white-maned warrior charges from the darkened portico and swings his sword against the statue's metal spine. It turns ponderously to deal with this distraction—a distraction which buys you the seconds you need to recover and leap to your feet. The white-haired adventurer is battering furiously at the statue, though each blow shatters slivers from his blade and does no harm at all to his opponent. He is mad with battle-lust. 'You damned devil!' he roars. I'll not stand

idly by and watch you take another life!' Even when the statue lifts its massive fists, he does not flinch. He is utterly transformed now—you no longer recognize him as the cringing figure you scorned. As the death blow descends, his expression is one of defiant rage.

The statue lumbers around to face you once more. Its hands are wet with blood and brains. You have seen the futility of swords against this foe—will you run from it (turn to **223**) or, if you still have the spell, will you cast Burning Tiger (turn to **140**)?

300

You find a breach in the high wall that encloses the mansion grounds. Scrambling over the chunks of weathered rubble, you enter a weed-choked garden. The long grass sways eerily, tinted an unnatural swart hue by the cold moonlight. You tread across a marshy lawn towards the mansion. Beside the crooked portico, like a grim and implacable sentinel, stands the bronze statue of a muscular warrior. It is pitted and eaten by centuries of corrosion. The face stares out, pock-marked and blind, as you draw near.

You look past the statue into the gaping black doorway of the mansion. A tangle of vines overhangs it like a giant cobweb. You need no sorcery to sense the danger here.

If you enter the mansion, turn to **216**. If you investigate the statue more closely first, turn to **61**. If you leave and head along the Avenue of Sphinxes, turn to **120**.

301

With a choked cry, you sink to your knees in a trembling heap. You feel something reach out and clutch at your robe. You shudder, but dare not look up. The unseen hands find your backpack and rummage within, removing two items before retreating into the lightless dark once more. (Cross off any two items except your sword, Orb of Illumination, or bag of gold.)

Numbing terror threatens to overwhelm you, but you fight back and finally manage to speak the mystic phrases needed to activate your Mind Shield spell. The eerie clamour all about you seems less appalling now. Turn to **19**.

302

Will you cast:

A Mirage spell?	Turn to **124**
A Gust of Wind spell?	Turn to **58**

If you have neither of these, you must either fight (turn to **229**) or try to escape (turn to **116**).

303

You make your way past the toppled Idol and along the passage. After a short distance you come into a round chamber with no other exits. On a .stone table in the centre of the room rests a large shield. It is made of something like turtle-shell, and reflects the light of the magical Orb with a purplish sheen. If you take this shield, turn to **69**. If you leave it and return to the plaza outside the temple, turn to **274**.

304

You stand at the end of the Avenue of Sphinxes. The night is cold, and you can smell salt-spray on the breeze. Crouched beside the pedestal of a fallen monument, you tensely watch the silent ruins around you. To your right there stands a particularly imposing edifice, once the mansion of a wealthy noble.

If you investigate the mansion, turn to **300**. If you head quickly south along the Avenue of Sphinxes, turn to **120**.

305

You wipe the blood from your sword and are just about to continue on into the city when you hear a low moan.

The sergeant is alive—just barely. He raises himself up on his elbow and beckons you closer.

If you stoop and listen to what he is trying to say, turn to **29**. If you leave him, turn to **48**.

306

Much to your consternation, the Orb is resting on the brink of the parapet. Even a light breeze would send it rolling off, to fall and shatter on the rough cobblestones far below. You reach forward, hardly daring to breathe, and gently close your fingers around it.

While you are repairing the cord that secures it, you glance down. A few Kappa are straggling southwards across the wet quadrangle. The moon is climbing high in the sky. The tide will be rolling in around the southerly ruins by now. You peer out across the broken rooftops, but the misty rain obscures any view of the sea.

As you return to the stairway, you notice a large block of greyish ice or crystal at the far end of the roof. If you go over and take a closer look, turn to **37**. If you go back down to the ground floor, turn to **241**.

307

The magical gale conjured by your spell blows up through the gap at the bottom of the sheet of glass. The harp sways tantalizingly, but the delicate thread does not break. Before you can think of another spell to try, you hear the loud creak of the gate hinges.

Turn to **141**.

308

At the end of the meandering tunnel you find a room strewn with mouldering skeletons. Many still wear scraps of decaying armour, or clutch rusting weapons in their fleshless hands.

You do not waste any time here, but walk along a corridor leading on from the room.

Turn to **219**.

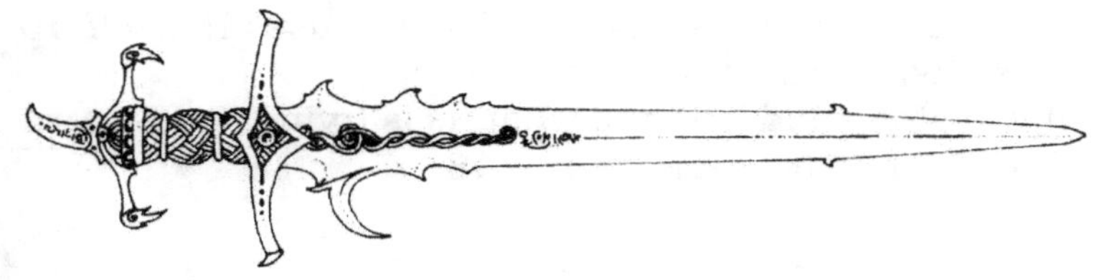

309

The Kappa order their sentinel crabs back. They want the pleasure of slaying you themselves.

| First KAPPA | VIGOUR 12 |
| Second KAPPA | VIGOUR 12 |

Roll two dice:

score 2 to 4	You are hit twice; lose 6 VIGOUR
score 5 to 7	You are hit once; lose 3 VIGOUR
score 8 to 12	One of the Kappa (you decide which) loses 3 VIGOUR

If you kill one, turn to **8**.

310

Using the astonishing power of the Eye, it is a simple matter to teleport yourself, Giru and the two guards back to the Academy. You materialize on a small cloister lawn and soon dozens of bemused scholars are gathering around you. You quickly make you way to the great hall where the High Council awaits you. Giru renders a full report and then steps up to take his seat with the others. 'We, the Master Scholars of the Academy of the Light of Truth, thank you for what you have done,' he says. 'You found yourself in the midst of a perilous adventure which no one had foreseen, yet you struggled on and managed to save the Eye of the Dragon from the Kappa's fell clutches. If is our feeling that the Eye should now be kept in a place of safety where its powers can be studied. But we cannot force you to relinquish it, nor would we choose to. Will you, then, entrust it to our care?'

You step up and place the glowing jewel on the table in front of him. Giru looks into your eyes. 'A wise decision,' he says. 'In the hands of a single individual, even one as noble as yourself, such power could only breed arrogance and evil.'

You do not disagree with that. 'There's a more important reason, though. You see, if I kept an item as powerful as the Eye, it would take all the fun out of adventuring.'

If you enjoyed *The Eye of the Dragon*, try these other classic adventure gamebooks by Dave Morris.

It is the dawn of the 24th century and the Earth is dying. Gaia, a satellite array designed to repair the effects of global warming, is out of control. A new Ice Age tightens its inexorable grip on the planet. Humanity is on the edge of extinction.

Mankind's last hope is the Heart of Volent, a strange meteorite which has already brought mutation and chaos to the world. Legend says that the one who finds it shall wield the power to reshape the universe.

As the ice sheets spread and the world slides towards the brink, you and a handful of bitter rivals compete in the race for the Heart. Only one can win. Are you ruthless and resourceful enough to claim the ultimate prize?

War is brewing between the kingdoms of Glorianne and Sidonia, a war waged for control of the territories of the New World. Galleons laden with gold ply the seas, and in their wake sail pirates and privateers eager for plunder.

Adrift in an open boat, you make your desperate bid to escape from the sadistic Captain Skarvench. You are determined to round up a crew, get yourself a ship, and set sail on a voyage of vengeance and justice. You are destined to face many perils: undead pirates, sea monsters, cursed ships, witches and ancient gods. And the greatest threat of all: the premonition of your own death at the hands of your hated foe.

DOWN AMONG THE DEAD MEN

The sole survivor of an expedition brings news of disaster. Your twin brother is lost in the trackless western sierra. Resolving to find out his fate, you leave the safety of your home far behind. Your quest takes you to lost jungle cities, across mountains and seas, and even into the depths of the underworld.

You will confront ghosts and gods, bargain for your life against wily demons, find allies and enemies among both the living and the dead. If you are brave enough to survive the dangers of the spirit-haunted western desert, you must still confront the wizard called Necklace of Skulls in a deadly contest whose stakes are nothing less than your own soul.

NECKLACE OF SKULLS

You have made a deadly enemy. Jafar, advisor to the Caliph, plans a coup that will put him on the throne of Baghdad. You are the only one who can warn the Caliph, but who will listen to a penniless adventurer? Especially as Jafar's assassins are scouring the city to find you.

You go in search of the fame and fortune that will give you the means to expose Jafar's treachery. Your travels take you to ghoul-haunted oases, magical palaces, lost cities of gold, and uncharted isles full of mystery and danger. Threatened by bandits, fire wizards, thieves and fearsome creatures, you must risk all in your determined quest to save the kingdom.

ONCE UPON A TIME IN ARABIA

FABLED LANDS

A sweeping fantasy role-playing campaign in gamebook form

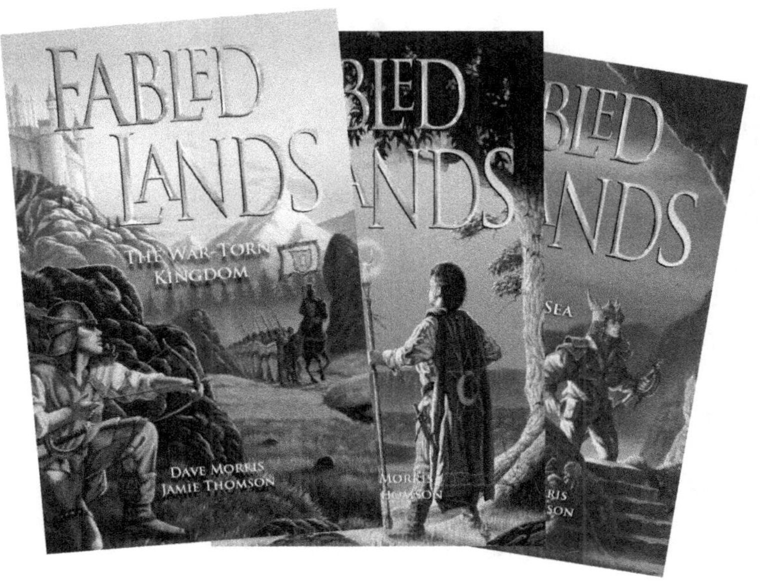

Set out on a journey of unlimited adventure!

FABLED LANDS is an epic interactive gamebook series with the scope of a massively multiplayer game world. You can choose to be an explorer, merchant, priest, scholar or soldier of fortune. You can buy a ship or a townhouse, join a temple, undertake desperate adventures in the wilderness or embroil yourself in court intrigues and the sudden violence of city backstreets. You can undertake missions that will earn you allies and enemies, or you can remain a free agent. With thousands of numbered sections to explore, the choices are all yours.

9 781909 905283